JACOB
HAVE I
LOVED

JACOB HAVE I LOVED

Katherine Paterson

Thomas Y. Crowell   New York

Copyright © 1980 by Katherine Paterson
All rights reserved. Printed in the United States of America.
No part of this book may be used or reproduced in any manner
whatsoever without written permission except in the case of
brief quotations embodied in critical articles and reviews.
For information address Thomas Y. Crowell Junior Books, 10 East 53rd Street,
New York, N.Y. 10022. Published simultaneously in Canada by
Fitzhenry & Whiteside Limited, Toronto.
Designed by Harriett Barton

Library of Congress Cataloging in Publication Data
Paterson, Katherine.   Jacob have I loved.

SUMMARY: Feeling deprived all her life of schooling,
friends, mother, and even her name by her twin sister,
Louise finally begins to find her identity.
[1. Twins—Fiction. 2. Brothers and sisters—
Fiction. 3. Chesapeake Bay region—Fiction]
I. Title.   PZ7.P273Jac 1980   [Fic]   80-668
ISBN 0-690-04078-4   ISBN 0-690-04079-2 (lib. bdg.)

2   3   4   5   6   7   8   9   10

131590

For

Gene Inyart Namovicz
I wish it were EMMA, *but, then,*
you already have two or three
copies of that.
With thanks and love.

ACKNOWLEDGMENTS

The impetus for this book came from reading William W. Warner's *Beautiful Swimmers: Watermen, Crabs and the Chesapeake Bay,* Little Brown and Company, 1976, which justly deserved the Pulitzer Prize it won the following year. Since then, there have been many people and books that have helped me learn more about life on the Chesapeake Bay. I should like especially to mention the Smith Island watermen I met at the Folk Life Festival at the Smithsonian: Mr. Harold G. Wheatley of Tangier Island, Virginia, and Dr. Varley Lang of Tunis Mills, Maryland. Dr. Lang, who is a writer and scholar as well as a Maryland waterman, was kind enough to read this manuscript. Any errors that remain are, of course, my fault and not his. His book about Maryland watermen entitled *Follow the Water,* John F. Blair, 1961, was also a great help to me.

Rass Island

As soon as the snow melts, I will go to Rass and fetch my mother. At Crisfield I'll board the ferry, climbing down into the cabin where the women always ride, but after forty minutes of sitting on the hard cabin bench, I'll stand up to peer out of the high forward windows, straining for the first sight of my island.

The ferry will be almost there before I can see Rass, lying low as a terrapin back on the faded olive water of the Chesapeake. Suddenly, though, the steeple of the Methodist Church will leap from the Bay, dragging up a cluster of white board houses. And then, almost at once, we will be in the harbor, tying up beside Captain Billy's unpainted two-story ferry house, which leans wearily against a long, low shed used for the captain's crab shipping business. Next door, but standing primly aloof in a coat of fierce green paint, is Kellam's General Store with the post office inside, and behind them, on a narrow spine of fast land, the houses and white picket fences of the village. There are only a few spindly trees. It is

1

the excess of snowball bushes that lends a semblance of green to every yard.

The dock onto which I'll step is part of a maze of docks. My eye could travel down the planking of any one of them and find at the end a shack erected by a waterman for storage and crab packing. If I arrive in late spring, the crab houses will be surrounded by slat floats that hold and protect peeler crabs in the water of the Bay until they have shed. Then the newly soft crabs will be packed in eelgrass and the boxes taken to Captain Billy's for shipping to the mainland.

More important than the crab houses, however, are the boats, tied along the docks. Though each has a personality as distinctive as the waterman who owns it, they look deceptively alike—a small cabin toward the bow, washboards wide enough for a man to stand on running from the point of the bow to the stern. In the belly of the hull, fore and aft of the engine are a dozen or so barrels waiting for the next day's catch, a spare crab pot or two, looking like a box made of chicken wire, and a few empty bait baskets. Near the winch that pulls the line of pots up from the floor of the Chesapeake is a large washtub. Into it each crab pot will be emptied and from it the legal-sized crabs—hard, peeler, and soft— will be culled from their smaller kin as well as from the blowfish, sea nettles, seaweed, shells, and garbage, all such unwelcome harvest as the Bay seems ever generous to offer up. On the stern, each boat bears its name. They are nearly all women's names, usually the name of the waterman's mother or grandmother, depending on how long the boat has been in the family.

The village, in which we Bradshaws lived for more than two hundred years, covers barely a third of our island's length. The rest is salt water marsh. As a child I secretly welcomed the first warm day of spring by yanking off my shoes and standing waist deep in the cordgrass to feel the cool mud squish up between my toes. I chose the spot with care, for cordgrass alone is rough enough to rip the skin, and ours often concealed a bit of curling tin or shards of glass or crockery or jagged shells not yet worn smooth by the tides. In my nostrils, the faint hay smell of the grass mingled with that of the brackish water of the Bay, while the spring wind chilled the tips of my ears and raised goosebumps along my arms. Then I would shade my eyes from the sun and search far across the water hoping to see my father's boat coming home.

I love Rass Island, although for much of my life, I did not think I did, and it is a pure sorrow to me that, once my mother leaves, there will be no one left there with the name of Bradshaw. But there were only the two of us, my sister, Caroline, and me, and neither of us could stay.

1

During the summer of 1941, every weekday morning at
the top of the tide, McCall Purnell and I would board
my skiff and go progging for crab. Call and I were right
smart crabbers, and we could always come home with
a little money as well as plenty of crab for supper. Call
was a year older than I and would never have gone crabbing with a girl except that his father was dead, so he
had no man to take him on board a regular crab boat.
He was, as well, a boy who had matured slowly, and
being fat and nearsighted, he was dismissed by most of
the island boys.

Call and I made quite a pair. At thirteen I was tall
and large boned, with delusions of beauty and romance.
He, at fourteen, was pudgy, bespectacled, and totally un-
sentimental.

"Call," I would say, watching dawn break crimson
over the Chesapeake Bay, "I hope I have a sky like this
the day I get married."

"Who would marry you?" Call would ask, not meanly,
just facing facts.

"Oh," I said one day, "I haven't met him yet."

"Then you ain't likely to. This is a right small island."

"It won't be an islander."

"Mr. Rice has him a girl friend in Baltimore."

I sighed. All the girls on Rass Island were half in love with Mr. Rice, one of our two high school teachers. He was the only relatively unattached man most of us had ever known. But Mr. Rice had let it get around that his heart was given to a lady from Baltimore.

"Do you suppose," I asked, as I poled the skiff, the focus of my romantic musings shifting from my own wedding day to Mr. Rice's, "do you suppose her parents oppose the marriage?"

"Why should they care?" Call, standing on the port washboard, had sighted the head of what seemed to be a large sea terrapin and was fixing on it a fierce concentration.

I shifted the pole to starboard. We could get a pretty little price for a terrapin of that size. The terrapin sensed the change in our direction and dove straight through the eelgrass into the bottom mud, but Call had the net waiting, so that when the old bull hit his hiding place, he was yanked to the surface and deposited into a waiting pail. Call grunted with satisfaction. We might make as much as fifty cents on that one catch, ten times the price of a soft blue crab.

"Maybe she's got some mysterious illness and doesn't want to be a burden to him."

"Who?"

"Mr. Rice's finance." I had picked up the word, but not the pronunciation from my reading. It was not in the spoken vocabulary of most islanders.

"His *what*?"

"The woman he's engaged to marry, stupid."

"How come you think she's sick?"

"Something is delaying the consumption of their union."

Call jerked his head around to give me one of his looks, but the washboards of a skiff are a precarious perch at best, so he didn't stare long enough to waste time or risk a dunking. He left me to what he presumed to be my looniness and gave his attention to the eelgrass. We were a good team on the water. I could pole a skiff quickly and quietly, and nearsighted as he was he could spy a crab by just a tip of the claw through grass and muck. He rarely missed one, and he knew I wouldn't jerk or swerve at the wrong moment. I'm sure that's why he stuck with me. I stuck with him not only because we could work well together, but because our teamwork was so automatic that I was free to indulge my romantic fantasies at the same time. That this part of my nature was wasted on Call didn't matter. He didn't have any friends but me, so he wasn't likely to repeat what I said to someone who might snicker. Call himself never laughed.

I thought of it as a defect in his character that I must try to correct, so I told him jokes. "Do you know why radio announcers have tiny hands?"

"Huh?"

"Wee paws for station identification," I would whoop.

"Yeah?"

"Don't you get it, Call? Wee paws. *Wee Paws.*" I let go the pole to shake my right hand at him. "You know, little hands—paws."

"You ain't never seen one."

"One what?"

"One radio announcer."

"No."

"Then how do you know how big their hands are?"

"I don't. It's a joke, Call."

"I don't see how it can be a joke if you don't even know if they have big hands or little hands. Suppose they really have big hands. Then you ain't even telling the truth. Then what happens to your joke?"

"It's just a joke, Call. It doesn't matter whether it's true or not."

"It matters to me. Why should a person think a lie's funny?"

"Never mind, Call. It doesn't matter."

But he went on, mumbling like a little old preacher about the importance of truth and how you couldn't trust radio announcers anymore.

You'd think I'd give up, but I didn't.

"Call, did you hear about the lawyer, the dentist, and the p-sychiatrist who died and went to heaven?"

"Was it a airplane crash?"

"No, Call. It's a joke."

"Oh, a joke."

7

"Yeah. You see, this lawyer and this dentist and this p-sychiatrist all die. And first the lawyer gets there. And Peter says—"

"Peter who?"

"Peter in the Bible. The Apostle Peter."

"He's dead."

"I know he's dead—"

"But you just said—"

"Just shut up and listen to the joke, Call. This lawyer comes to Peter, and he wants to get into heaven."

"A minute ago you said he was already in heaven."

"Well, he wasn't. He was just at the pearly gates, okay? Anyhow, he says he wants to get into heaven, and Peter says he's sorry but he's looked at the book and the lawyer was wicked and evil and cheated people. So he's got to go to hell."

"Does your mother know you use words like that?"

"Call, even the preacher talks about hell. Anyhow, this lawyer has to give up and go to hell. Then this dentist comes up and he wants to get into heaven, and Peter looks at his book and sees that this guy pulled people's teeth out just to get their money even when their teeth were perfectly good and he knew it."

"He did *what*?"

"Call, it doesn't matter."

"It don't matter that a dentist pulls out perfectly good teeth just to make money? That's awful. He ought to go to jail."

"Well, he went to hell for it."

"Pulling out perfectly good teeth—" he mumbled, pinching his own with the fingers of his left hand.

"Then the p-sychiatrist—"

"The what?"

I was an avid reader of *Time* magazine, which, besides the day-old Baltimore *Sun,* was our porthole on the world in those days, so although psychiatry was not yet a popular pastime, I was quite aware of the word, if not the fact that the p was silent. *Time* was probably the source of the joke I was laboring to recount.

"A p-sychiatrist is a doctor that works with people who are crazy."

"Why would you try to do anything with people who're crazy?"

"To get them well. To make their minds better. Good heavens." We paused to net a huge male crab, a true number one Jimmy, swimming doubled over a she-crab. He was taking her to the thick eelgrass, where she would shed for the last time and become a grown-up lady crab— a sook. When she was soft, there would be a proper crab wedding, of course, with the groom staying around to watch out for his bride until her shell was hard once more, and she could protect herself and her load of eggs on her own.

"Sorry, Mr. Jimmy," I said, "no wedding bells for you."

Now this old Jimmy didn't much like being deprived of his sweetheart, but Call pinched him from behind and threw each of them in a separate bucket. She was a rank peeler—that is, it wouldn't be more than a couple of hours before she shed. Our bucket for rank peelers was almost full. It was a good day on the water.

"Well, like I was saying, this p-sychiatrist comes up to Peter, and Peter looks him up in the book of judgment and finds out he's been mean to his wife and kids and tells him to go to hell."

"What?"

I ignored him. Otherwise I'd never get the story finished. "So the p-sychiatrist starts to leave, and then Peter says all of a sudden: 'Hey! Did you say you were a p-sychiatrist?' And the guy says, 'Yes, I did.' " I was talking so fast now, I was almost out of breath. "And Peter says, 'I think we can use you around here after all. You see, we got this problem. God thinks he's Franklin D. Roosevelt.' "

"God *what*?"

"You know when people are crazy they think they're somebody important—like Napoleon or something."

"But, Wheeze, God *is* important."

"It's a joke, Call."

"How can it be a joke? There ain't neither funny about it." He had broken into a waterman's emphatic negative.

"Call, it's funny because Franklin D. Roosevelt has got too big for his britches. Like he's better than God or something."

"But that's not what you said. You said—"

"I know what I said. But you gotta understand politics."

"Well, what kinda joke is that? Fiddle." Call's cuss

words were taught to him by his sainted grandmother and tended to be as quaint as the clothes she made for him.

When the sun was high and our stomachs empty, Call stepped off the washboards into the boat. I shipped the pole and moved up with him to the forward thwart, where we put the oars into the locks and rowed the boat out of the eelgrass into deeper water and around to the harbor.

Captain Billy's son Otis ran the crab shipping part of his father's business, while his father and two brothers ran the ferry. We sold our soft crabs, peelers, and the terrapin to Otis, then split the money and the hard crabs. Call ran home to dinner, and I rowed back around the island as far as the South Gut, where I traded oars for the pole and poled the rest of the way home. The South Gut was a little ditch of water, one of many that criss-crossed Rass, and a natural garbage dump. The summer before, Call and I had cleaned it out (it had been clogged with rusting cans and crab pots, even old mattress springs) so I could pole the skiff through it all the way to my own backyard. Rass might be short on trees, but there was a loblolly pine sapling and a fig tree that my mother had planted on our side of the gut, as well as an orphan cedar on the other. I hitched my skiff to the pine and started at a trot for the back porch, a bucket of hard crabs in one hand and a fistful of money in the other.

My grandmother caught me before I got to the door. "Louise Bradshaw! Don't you go coming in the house dirty like that. Oh, my blessed, what a mess! Susan," she called back in to my mother, "she's full ruined every scrap of clothes she owns."

Rather than argue, I put my crab bucket and money on the edge of the porch and stepped out of my overalls. Underneath I had on my oldest cotton dress.

"Hang them overhalls on the back line, now."

I obeyed, pinning the straps securely to the clothesline. Immediately, the breeze took them straight out, as though Peter Pan had donned them to fly across our yard toward never-never land across the Bay.

I was humming with goodwill, "Come, Thou Fount of every blessing, tune my heart to sing Thy grace . . ." My grandmother was not going to get me today. I'd had a right smart haul.

Caroline was shelling peas at the kitchen table. I smiled at my sister benevolently.

"Mercy, Wheeze, you stink like a crab shanty."

I gritted my teeth, but the smile was still framing them. "Two dollars," I said to my mother at the stove, "two dollars and forty-five cents."

She beamed at me and reached over the propane stove for the pickle crock, where we kept the money. "My," she said, "that was a good morning. By the time you wash up, we'll be ready to eat."

I liked the way she did that. She never suggested that I was dirty or that I stank. Just—"By the time you wash up—" She was a real lady, my mother.

While we were eating, she asked me to go to Kellam's afterward to get some cream and butter. I knew what that meant. It meant that I had made enough money that she could splurge and make she-crab soup for supper. She wasn't an islander, but she could make the best she-crab soup on Rass. My grandmother always complained that no good Methodist would ever put spirits into food. But my mother was undaunted. Our soup always had a spoonful or two of her carefully hoarded sherry ladled into it. My grandmother complained, but she never left any in the bowl.

I was sitting there, basking in the day, thinking how pleased my father would be to come home from crabbing and smell his favorite soup, bathing my sister and grand-mother in kindly feelings that neither deserved, when Caroline said, "I haven't got anything to do but practice this summer, so I've decided to write a book about my life. Once you're known," she explained carefully as though some of us were dim-witted, "once you're famous, information like that is very valuable. If I don't get it down now, I may forget." She said all this in that voice of hers that made me feel slightly nauseated, the one she used when she came home from spending all Saturday going to the mainland for her music lessons, where she'd been told for the billionth time how gifted she was.

I excused myself from the table. The last thing I needed to hear that day was the story of my sister's life, in which I, her twin, was allowed a very minor role.

2

If my father had not gone to France in 1918 and collected a hip full of German shrapnel, Caroline and I would never have been born. As it was, he did go to war, and when he returned, his childhood sweetheart had married someone else. He worked on other men's boats as strenuously as his slowly healing body would let him, eking out a meager living for himself and his widowed mother. It was almost ten years before he was strong enough to buy a boat of his own and go after crabs and oysters like a true Rass waterman.

One fall, before he had regained his full strength, a young woman came to teach in the island school (three classrooms plus a gymnasium of sorts), and, somehow, though I was never able to understand it fully, the elegant little schoolmistress fell in love with my large, red-faced, game-legged father, and they were married.

What my father needed more than a wife was sons. On Rass, sons represented wealth and security. What my mother bore him was girls, twin girls. I was the elder by a few minutes. I always treasured the thought of those

14

minutes. They represented the only time in my life when I was the center of everyone's attention. From the moment Caroline was born, she snatched it all for herself.

When my mother and grandmother told the story of our births, it was mostly of how Caroline had refused to breathe. How the midwife smacked and prayed and cajoled the tiny chest to move. How the cry of joy went up at the first weak wail—"no louder than a kitten's mew."

"But where was I?" I once asked. "When everyone was working over Caroline, where was I?"

A cloud passed across my mother's eyes, and I knew that she could not remember. "In the basket," she said. "Grandma bathed you and dressed you and put you in the basket."

"Did you, Grandma?"

"How should I know?" she snapped. "It was a long time ago."

I felt cold all over, as though I was the newborn infant a second time, cast aside and forgotten.

Ten days after our birth, despite the winter wind and a threat of being iced in, my mother took Caroline on the ferry to the hospital in Crisfield. My father had no money for doctors and hospitals, but my mother was determined. Caroline was so tiny, so fragile, she must be given every chance of life. My mother's father was alive in those days. He may have paid the bill. I've never known. What I do know is that my mother went eight or ten times each day to the hospital to nurse Caroline, believing that the milk of a loving mother would supply a healing power that even doctors could not.

But what of me? "Who took care of me while you were gone?" The story always left the other twin, the stronger twin, washed and dressed and lying in a basket. Clean and cold and motherless.

Again the vague look and smile. "Your father was here and your grandmother."

"Was I a good baby, Grandma?"

"No worse than most, I reckon."

"What did I do, Grandma? Tell me about when I was a baby."

"How can I remember? It's been a long time."

My mother, seeing my distress, said, "You were a good baby, Louise. You never gave us a minute's worry." She meant it to comfort me, but it only distressed me further. Shouldn't I have been at least a minute's worry? Wasn't it all the months of worry that had made Caroline's life so dear to them all?

When Caroline and I were two months old, my mother brought her back to the island. By then I had grown fat on tinned milk formula. Caroline continued at my mother's breast for another twelve months. There is a rare snapshot of the two of us sitting on the front stoop the summer we were a year and a half old. Caroline is tiny and exquisite, her blonde curls framing a face that is glowing with laughter, her arms outstretched to whoever is taking the picture. I am hunched there like a fat dark shadow, my eyes cut sideways toward Caroline, thumb in mouth, the pudgy hand covering most of my face.

The next winter we both had whooping cough. My mother thinks that I was sick enough to have a croup tent set up. But everyone remembers that Captain Billy got the ferry out at 2:00 A.M. to rush Caroline and my mother to the hospital.

We went that way through all the old childhood diseases except for chicken pox. We both had a heavy case of that, but only I still sport the scars. That mark on the bridge of my nose is a chicken pox scar. It was more noticeable when I was thirteen than it is now. Once my father referred to me teasingly as "Old Scarface" and looked perfectly bewildered when I burst into tears.

I suppose my father was used to treating me with a certain roughness, not quite as he would have treated a son, but certainly differently from the way he treated Caroline. My father, like nearly every man on our island, was a waterman. This meant that six days a week, long before dawn he was in his boat. From November to March, he was tonging for oysters, and from late April into the fall, he was crabbing. There are few jobs in this world more physically demanding than the work of those men who choose to follow the water. For one slightly lame man alone on a boat, the work was more than doubled. He needed a son and I would have given anything to be that son, but on Rass in those days, men's work and women's work were sharply divided, and a waterman's boat was not the place for a girl.

17

When I was six my father taught me how to pole a skiff so I could net crabs in the eelgrass near the shore. That was my consolation for not being allowed to go aboard the *Portia Sue* as his hand. As pleased as I was to have my own little skiff, it didn't make up for his refusal to take me on his boat. I kept praying to turn into a boy, I loved my father's boat with such a passion. He had named it after my mother's favorite character from Shakespeare to please her, but he had insisted on the Sue. My mother's name is Susan. In all likelihood he was the only waterman on the Chesapeake Bay whose boat was named for a woman lawyer out of Shakespeare.

My father was not educated in the sense that my mother was. He had dropped out of the island school at twelve to follow the water. I think he would have taken easily to books, but he came home at night too tired to read. I can remember my mother sometimes reading aloud to him. He would sit in his chair, his head back, his eyes closed, but he wasn't asleep. As a child, I always suspected he was imagining. Perhaps he was.

Although our house was one of the smaller of the forty or so houses on the island, for several years we owned the only piano. It came to us on the ferry after my mainland grandfather died. I think Caroline and I were about four when it arrived. She says she remembers meeting it at the dock and following while six men helped my father roll it on a dolly to our house, for there were no trucks or cars on the island.

Caroline also says that she began at once to pick out

tunes by ear and make up songs for herself. It may be true. I can hardly recall a time when Caroline was not playing the piano well enough to accompany herself while she sang.

My mother not being an islander and the islanders not being acquainted with pianos, no one realized at the beginning the effect of damp salt air on the instrument. Within a few weeks it was lugubriously out of tune. My inventive mother solved this problem by going to the mainland and finding a Crisfield piano tuner who could also give lessons. He came by ferry once a month and taught a half-dozen island youngsters, including Caroline and me, on our piano. During the Depression he was glad to get the extra work. For food, a night's lodging, and the use of our piano, he tuned it and gave Caroline and me free lessons. The rest, children of the island's slightly more affluent, paid fifty cents a lesson. During the month each paid twenty cents a week to practice on our piano. In those days, an extra eighty cents a week was a princely sum.

I was no better or worse than most. We all seemed to get as far as "Country Gardens" and stay there. Caroline, on the other hand, was playing Chopin by the time she was nine. Sometimes people would stand outside the house just to listen while she practiced. Whenever I am tempted to dismiss the poor or uneducated for their vulgar tastes, I see the face of old Auntie Braxton, as she stands stock still in front of our picket fence, lips parted to reveal her almost toothless gums, eyes shining, drinking in a polonaise as though it were heavenly nourishment.

By the time we were ten, it became apparent, though, that Caroline's true gift was her voice. She had always been able to sing clearly and in tune, but the older she grew, the lovelier the tune became. The mainland county schoolboard, which managed the island school more by neglect than anything else, suddenly, and without explanation, sent the school a piano the year Caroline and I were in the fifth grade, and the next year, by what could only have been the happiest of coincidences, the new teacher appointed as half of the high school staff was a young man who not only knew how to play a piano but had the talent and strength of will to organize a chorus. Caroline was, of course, his inspiration and focal point. There was little to entertain the island youth, so we sang. And because we sang everyday and Mr. Rice was a gifted teacher, we sang surprisingly well for children who had known little music in their lives.

We went to a contest on the mainland the spring we were thirteen and might have won except that when the judges realized our chief soloist was not yet in high school, we were disqualified. Mr. Rice was furious, but we children figured that the mainland schools were too embarrassed to be beaten out by islanders and so made up a rule to save their faces.

Sometime before that Mr. Rice had persuaded my parents that Caroline should have voice lessons. At first they refused, not because of the time and effort it would take to get Caroline to the mainland every Saturday, but because there was no money. But Mr. Rice was determined. He took Caroline to the college in Salisbury and had her sing for the head of the music department. Not only did the man agree to take Caroline on as a private pupil, he waived the fee. Even then the two round-trip tickets on the ferry plus the taxi fare to Salisbury put an unbelievable strain on the weekly budget, but Caroline is the kind of person other people sacrifice for as a matter of course.

I was proud of my sister, but that year, something began to rankle beneath the pride. Life begins to turn upside down at thirteen. I know that now. But at the time I thought the blame for my unhappiness must be fixed—on Caroline, on my grandmother, on my mother, even on myself. Soon I was able to blame the war.

3

Even I who read *Time* magazine from cover to cover every week was unprepared for Pearl Harbor. The machinations of European powers and the funny mustached German dictator were as remote to our island in the fall of 1941 as *Silas Marner,* which sapped our energies through eighth-grade English.

There were hints, but at the time I didn't make sense of them: Mr. Rice's great concern for "peace on earth" as we began at Thanksgiving to prepare for our Christmas concert; overhearing a partial conversation between my parents in which my father pronounced himself "useless," to which my mother replied, "Thank the Lord."

It was not a phrase my mother often used, but it was a true island expression. Rass had lived in the fear and mercy of the Lord since the early nineteenth century, when Joshua Thomas, "The Parson of the Islands," won every man, woman, and child of us to Methodism. Old Joshua's stamp remained upon us—Sunday school and Sunday service morning and evening, and on Wednesday night prayer meeting where the more fervent would stand to witness to the Lord's mercies of the preceding week and all the sick and straying would be held up in prayer before the Throne of Grace.

We kept the Sabbath. That meant no work, no radio, no fun on Sunday. But for some reason my parents were out on the Sunday afternoon that was December 7, my grandmother was snoring loudly from her bed, and Caroline was reading the deadly dull Sunday school paper— our only permitted reading on the Sabbath other than the Bible itself. So I, bored almost to madness, had wandered into the living room and turned on the radio, very low so that no one could hear, and pressed my ear against the speaker.

"The Japanese in a predawn surprise attack have destroyed the American fleet at Pearl Harbor. I repeat. The White House has confirmed that the Japanese . . ."

I knew by the chill that went through my body that it meant war. All my magazine reading and overheard remarks fell at once into a grotesque but understandable pattern. I rushed up to our room where Caroline, still innocent and golden, lay stomach down on her bed reading.

"Caroline!"

She didn't even look up. "Caroline!" I ripped the paper from under her hands. "The Japanese have invaded America!"

"Oh, Wheeze, for pity sake." And hardly looking up, she grabbed for her paper. I was used to her ignoring me, but this time I would not allow it. I snatched her arm and dragged her off her bed and down the stairs to the radio. I turned the volume up full. The fact that the Japanese had attacked Hawaii rather than invaded the continental United States was a distinction that neither of us bothered to quibble over. She, like me, was totally caught by the tone of fear that even the smooth baritone of the announcer's voice could not conceal. Caroline's eyes went wide, and, as we listened, she did something she had never done before. She took my hand. We stood there, squeezing each other's hand to the point of pain.

That is how our parents found us. There was no remonstrance for having broken the Fourth Commandment. The crime of the Japanese erased all lesser sinning. The four of us huddled together before the radio set. It was one of those pointed ones that remind you of a brown wood church, with long oval windows over a cloth-covered speaker.

At six, Grandma woke, hungry and petulant. No one had given any thought to food. How could one think of supper when the world had just gone up in flames? Finally, my mother went to the kitchen and made plates of cold meat and leftover potato salad, which she brought to the three of us hunched about the set. She even brought coffee for us all. Grandma insisted on being served properly at the table. Caroline and I had never drunk coffee in our lives, and the fact that our mother served us coffee that night made us both realize that our secure, ordinary world was forever in the past.

Just as I was about to take my first solemn sip, the announcer said, "We pause, now, for station identification." I nearly choked. The world had indeed gone mad.

Within a few days we learned that Mr. Rice had volunteered for the army and would be leaving for the war soon after Christmas. In chorus one morning the irony of celebrating the birth of the Prince of Peace suddenly seemed too much. I raised my hand.

"Yes, Louise?"

"Mr. Rice," I said, standing and dramatically darkening my voice to what I imagined to be the proper tone for mourning, "Mr. Rice, I have a proposal to make." There were a few snickers at my choice of words, but I ignored them. "I feel, sir, that under the circumstances, we should cancel Christmas."

Mr. Rice's right eyebrow shot up. "Do you want to explain that, Louise?"

"How," I asked, my glance sweeping about to catch the amused looks of the others, "how dare we celebrate while around the world thousands are suffering and dying?" Caroline was staring down at her desk, her cheeks red.

Mr. Rice cleared his throat. "Thousands were suffering and dying when Christ was born, Louise." He was clearly discomfited by my behavior. I was sorry now that I had begun but was in too deeply to retreat.

"Yes," I agreed grandly. "But the world has not seen, neither has it heard, such a tragic turn of events as we face in this our time."

Tiny little one-syllable explosions went off about the room like a string of Chinese firecrackers. Mr. Rice looked stern.

My face was burning. I'm not sure whether I was more embarrassed by the sound of my own voice or the snorts of my schoolmates. I sat down, my whole body aflame. The snorts broke into open laughter. Mr. Rice tapped his baton on his music stand to restore order. I thought he might try to explain what I had meant, would try in some way to mediate for me, but he said only, "Now then, let's try it once more from the beginning—"

"God rest ye merry, gentlemen, let nothing you dismay," sang everyone except me. I was afraid if I opened my mouth, I might let go the enormous sob that was lurking there, right at the top of my throat.

It was nearly dark when school got out that afternoon. I rushed out before anyone could catch up with me and walked, not home, but across the length of the marsh on the one high path to the very southern tip of the island. The mud had a frozen brown crust and the cordgrass was weighed down by ice. The wind cut mercilessly across the barren end of Rass, but the hot shame and indignation inside me made me forget the wind as I walked. I was right. I knew I was right, so why had they all laughed? And why had Mr. Rice let them? He hadn't even tried to explain what I meant to the others. It was only when I came to the end of the path and sat down upon a giant stump of driftwood and stared at the sickly winter moon waveringly reflected on the black water that I realized how cold I was and began to cry.

I should not forget that it was Caroline who came and found me there. Sitting on the stump, my back to the swamp and the village, I was crying aloud, so that I did not even hear the crunch of her galoshes.

"Wheeze."

I jerked around, angry to be found out.

"It's past time for your supper," she said.

"I'm not hungry."

"Oh, Wheeze," she said. "It's too cold to stay out here."

"I'm not coming back. I'm running away."

"Well, you can't run away tonight," she said. "There's no ferry until tomorrow morning. You might as well come in and have supper and get warm."

That was Caroline. I would hope for tears and pleadings. She offered facts. But they were facts I couldn't argue with. It would be next to impossible to run away in a skiff at any time of year. I sighed, wiped my face on the back of my hand, and rose to follow her. Even though I could have walked the path blindfolded, I felt foolishly grateful for the homely bobbing comfort of her flashlight.

The watermen of Rass had their own time system. Four-thirty was suppertime winter and summer. So when Caroline and I walked in, our parents and grandmother were already eating. I expected a reprimand from my father or a tongue-lashing from my grandmother, but to my relief they simply nodded as we came in. Mother

27

got up to bring us some hot food from the stove, which she put before us when we had washed and sat down. Caroline must have told them what had happened at school. I was torn between gratitude that they should sympathize and anger that they should know.

The school concert was Saturday night. Sunday was the only day the men did not get up before dawn, and therefore Saturday night was the only night anyone of the island would consider spending in a frivolous manner. I didn't want to go, but it would have been harder to stay away and imagine what people were saying about me than to go and face them.

The boys had helped Mr. Rice rig up footlights, really a row of naked bulbs behind reflectors cut from tin cans, but they gave the tiny stage at the end of the gymnasium a magical distance from the audience. As I stood there on the stage floor in front of the risers, I could barely make out the familiar features of my parents in the center of the second row of chairs. I felt as if those of us on the stage were floating in another layer of the world, removed from those below. When I squinted my eyes, the people all blurred like a film that has jumped the sprockets and is racing untended through the machine. I think I sang most of the program with my eyes squinted. It was a very comforting feeling thus to remove myself from the world I imagined was laughing at me.

Betty Jean Boyd sang the solo for "O Holy Night," and I hardly flinched when she went flat on the first "shining." Betty Jean was considered to have a lovely voice. In any other generation on Rass she would have been worshiped for it, flat as it was, but in my day on Rass, everyone had heard Caroline sing. No one should have had to bear that comparison. Poor Betty Jean. I was puzzled that Mr. Rice should give her this solo. Caroline had sung it last year. Everyone would remember. But this year Mr. Rice had chosen a different solo for Caroline, a very simple one. I had been angry the first time he had sung it over for us. Caroline's voice, after all, was our school treasure. Why had he given the showy song to Betty Jean and a strange thin melody to Caroline?

Now Mr. Rice left the piano and stood before us, his arms tense, his long fingers slightly curved. His dark eyes traveled back and forth, willing every eye to meet his. There were a few polite coughs from the shadowy darkness behind him. It was time. In just a few seconds it would begin. I didn't dare to shift my gaze from Mr. Rice's face to Caroline's head, two rows behind and to the right of me in the back row, but my stomach knotted for her.

Mr. Rice's hands went down, and from the center of the back row Caroline's voice came suddenly like a single beam of light across the darkness.

I wonder as I wander out under the sky
Why Jesus the Savior did come for to die
For poor on'ry people like you and like I
I wonder as I wander—out under the sky.

29

It was a lonely, lonely sound, but so clear, so beautiful that I tightened my arms against my sides to keep from shaking, perhaps shattering. Then we were all singing, better than we had all night, better than we ever had, suddenly judged, damned, and purged in Caroline's light.

She sang once more by herself, repeating the words of the first verse so quietly that I knew surely I would shatter when she went up effortlessly, sweetly, and oh, so softly, to the high G, holding it just a few seconds longer than humanly possible and then returning to the last few notes and to silence.

A sharp report of applause suddenly rattled the room like gunfire. I jumped, first startled by the sound and then angered. I looked from the dark noisy blur to Mr. Rice, but he was already turning to take a bow. He motioned Caroline to step down and come forward, which she did. And when she turned to go back to her place, I was disgusted to see her dimpled and smiling. She was pleased with herself. It was the same expression she wore when she had thoroughly trounced me in checkers.

When we left the gymnasium, the stars were so bright, they pulled me up into the sky like powerful magnets. I walked, my head back, my own nearly flat chest pressed up against the bosom of heaven, dizzied by the winking brilliance of the night. "I wonder as I wander . . ."

Perhaps I would have drowned in wonder if Caroline, walking ahead with my parents, had not turned and called my name sharply. "Wheeze, you better watch out walking that way," she said. "You're likely to break your neck." She had now moved beyond my parents in the narrow street and was walking backward, the better, I suppose, to observe me.

"Better watch out yourself," I snapped, annoyed and embarrassed to be so yanked away from the stars. I realized suddenly how cold the wind had become. She laughed merrily and, still walking backward, doubled her speed. She was not likely to run into anything. She never stumbled or bumped into things. That, she seemed to be saying, was what I did—often enough for both of us.

Grandma was prone to arthritis and did not go out on a winter's night, even to prayer meeting. So once home, we had to tell her all about the concert. Caroline did most of the talking, singing a snatch of this or that to remind Grandma of a carol she claimed never to have heard before.

"Did you sing the Holy Night one again?"

"No, Grandma, remember, I told you Betty Jean Boyd was doing that this year."

"Why was that? She can't half sing like you can."

"Caroline sang a different one this year, Mother." My mother was making cocoa for us and calling in a word here and there from the kitchen. "Betty Jean sounded very sweet."

Caroline gave me a look and snorted out loud. I knew she was expecting me to contradict Momma, but I wasn't going to. If Caroline wanted to be snobbish about Betty Jean, she could do it on her own.

Caroline had begun to imitate Betty Jean's singing of "O Holy Night." It was almost perfect, just a fraction flatter and shakier than Betty Jean's voice had been, the o's and ah's parodies of Betty Jean's pretentious ones. She ended the performance with a mournful shriek more than a little off pitch and looked around, grinning for her family's approval.

All the way through I had expected my parents to stop her, invoking, if nothing else, the nearness of the neighbors. But no one had. And now, she had finished and was waiting for our applause. It came in the form of a smile working at the firm corners of my father's mouth. Caroline laughed happily. It was all she desired.

Surely Momma would protest. Instead she handed Grandma a cup to drink in her chair. "Here's your cocoa, Mother," she said. Caroline and I went to the table for ours, Caroline still smiling. I had a burning desire to hit her in the mouth, but I controlled myself.

That night I lay in bed with an emptiness chewing away inside of me. I said my prayers, trying to push it away with ritual, but it kept oozing back round the worn edges of the words. I had deliberately given up "Now I lay me down to sleep" two years before as being too babyish a prayer and had been using since then the Lord's Prayer attached to a number of formula "God blesses." But that night "Now I lay me" came back unbidden in the darkness.

32

Now I lay me down to sleep,
I pray the Lord my soul to keep.
If I should die before I wake,
I pray the Lord my soul to take.

"If I should die . . ." It didn't push back the emptiness. It snatched and tore at it, making the hole larger and darker. "If I should die . . ." I tried to shake the words away with "Yea, though I walk through the valley of the shadow of death, I shall fear no evil, for behold, thou art with me . . ."

There was something about the thought of God being with me that made me feel more alone than ever. It was like being with Caroline.

She was so sure, so present, so easy, so light and gold, while I was all gray and shadow. I was not ugly or monstrous. That might have been better. Monsters always command attention, if only for their freakishness. My parents would have wrung their hands and tried to make it up to me, as parents will with a handicapped or especially ugly child. Even Call, his nose too large for his small face, had a certain satisfactory ugliness. And his mother and grandmother did their share of worrying about him. But I had never caused my parents "a minute's worry." Didn't they know that worry proves you care? Didn't they realize that I needed their worry to assure myself that I was worth something?

I worried about them. I feared for my father's safety everytime there was a storm on the Bay, and for my mother's whenever she took the ferry to the mainland. I read magazine articles in the school library on health and gave them mental physical examinations and tested the health of their marriage. "Can this marriage succeed?" Probably not. They had nothing in common as far as I could tell from the questionnaires I read. I even worried about Caroline, though why should I bother when everyone else spent their lives fretting over her?

I longed for the day when they would have to notice me, give me all the attention and concern that was my due. In my wildest daydreams there was a scene taken from the dreams of Joseph. Joseph dreamed that one day all his brothers and his parents as well would bow down to him. I tried to imagine Caroline bowing down to me. At first, of course, she laughingly refused, but then a giant hand descended from the sky and shoved her to her knees. Her face grew dark. "Oh, Wheeze," she began to apologize. "Call me no longer Wheeze, but Sara Louise," I said grandly, smiling in the darkness, casting off the nickname she had diminished me with since we were two.

4

"I hate the water."

I didn't even bother to look up from my book. Grandma had two stock phrases. The first was "I love the Lord," and the second, "I hate the water." I had grown fully immune to both by the time I was eight.

"What time's the ferry due?"

"The same time as always, Grandma." I wished only to be left to my book, which was a deliciously scary one about some children who had been captured by a bunch of pirates in the West Indies. It was my mother's. All the books were hers except the extra Bibles.

"Don't be sassy."

I sighed and put down my book and said with greatly exaggerated patience, "The ferry is due about four, Grandma."

"Doubt but there's a northwest wind," she said mournfully. "Likely to be headed into the wind all the way in." She rocked her chair slowly back and forth with her eyes closed. Or almost closed. I usually had the feeling she was watching through slits. "Where's Truitt?"

"Daddy's working on the boat, Grandma."

She opened her eyes wide and sat up straight. "Not tonging?"

"Tonging's done, Grandma. It's April." It was spring vacation, and here I was sitting all day with a cranky old woman.

She settled back. I thought she might tell me not to be sassy once more for good measure, but instead she said, "That ferry of Billy's is too old. One of these days it's going to sink right there in the middle of the Bay, and no one will find neither plank of it never again."

I knew Grandma's fears were idle, but they stirred up a little fuzz ball of fear in my stomach. "Grandma," I said, as much to myself as to her, "it's got to be okay. Government's always checking it out. Ferryboat's got to be safe or it won't get a license. Government controls it."

She sniffed loudly. "Franklin D. Roosevelt think he can control the whole Chesapeake Bay? Ain't no government can control that water."

God thinks he's Franklin D. Roosevelt.

"What are you grinning about? Ain't nothing to grin about."

I pulled in my cheeks in an attempt to appear solemn. "You want some coffee, Grandma?" If I made her some coffee, it would distract her, and maybe she'd let me get back to my book in peace.

I slipped my book under the sofa cushion because it had a picture of a great sailing vessel on the front. I didn't want Grandma upset because I was reading a book about the water. The women of my island were not supposed to love the water. Water was the wild, untamed kingdom of our men. And though water was the element in which our tiny island lived and moved and had its being, the women resisted its power over their lives as a wife might pretend to ignore the existence of her husband's mistress. For the men of the island, except for the preacher and the occasional male teacher, the Bay was an all-consuming passion. It ruled their waking hours, sapped their bodily strength, and from time to tragic time claimed their mortal flesh.

I suppose I knew that there was no future for me on Rass. How could I face a lifetime of passive waiting? Waiting for the boats to come in of an afternoon, waiting in a crab house for the crabs to shed, waiting at home for children to be born, waiting for them to grow up, waiting, at last, for the Lord to take me home.

I gave Grandma her coffee and stood by while she noisily sucked in air and coffee. "Not enough sugar."

I whipped the sugar bowl out from behind my back. She was clearly annoyed that I'd been able to anticipate her complaint. I could see on her face that she was trying to decide how to shift to something that I wouldn't be prepared for. "Hmm," she said finally in a squeaky little tone and spooned two heaping measures of sugar into her cup. She didn't thank me, but I hadn't expected thanks. I was so delighted to have outsmarted her that I forgot myself and began whistling "Praise the Lord and Pass the Ammunition" as I returned the sugar bowl to the kitchen.

"Whistling women and crowing hens never come to no good end."

"Oh, I don't know, Grandma, we might be terrific in a circus freak show."

She was clearly shocked but couldn't seem to put her finger on my specific sin. "Thou shalt not—thou shalt not—"

"Whistle?"

"Sass!" She almost screamed. I had clearly gotten the best of her, so I sobered to an elaborate caricature of humility. "Can I get you anything else, Grandma?"

She humphed and hemmed and slurped her coffee without answering, but as soon as I'd gotten my book again and was settled down on the couch and reading, she said, "It's onto four o'clock."

I pretended not to hear.

"Ain't you going down for the ferry?"

"I hadn't thought to."

"It wouldn't hurt you to think a little. Your mother's likely to have heavy groceries."

"Caroline's with her, Grandma."

"You know full well that little child ain't got the strength to carry heavy groceries."

I could have said several things but all of them were rude, so I kept my mouth shut.

"Why do you look at me like that?" she asked.

"Like what?"

"With bullets in your eyes. Like you want to shoot me dead. All I want you to do is help your poor mother."

It was useless to argue. I took the book upstairs and hid it in my underwear drawer. Grandma was less likely to poke around in there. She considered modern female undergarments indecent and if not precisely "of the devil," certainly in that vicinity. I got a jacket, as the wind would be chilly, and went downstairs. When I reached the front door, the rocking stopped.

"Where you think you're going?"

Fury began to swoosh up inside me. I kept my voice as flat as I could and said, "Down to meet the ferry, Grandma. Remember? You said I should go and help Momma bring back the groceries."

She looked strangely blank. "Well, hurry," she said at last, beginning to rock again. "I don't favor waiting here by myself."

A small crowd of islanders had come by foot or bicycle and were already waiting the arrival of the ferry. They greeted me as I approached, pulling the red metal wagon that we used for hauling.

"Your Momma coming in?"

"Yes, Miss Letty. She had to take Caroline to the doctor."

Sympathetic looks all round. "That child has always been so delicate."

It was useless to withhold information; besides, for once, I didn't care. "She had an earache, and Nurse thought she ought to go have Dr. Walton check it."

Heads shook knowingly. "You can't be too careful 'bout the earache."

"Surely cannot. Remember, Lettice, when little Buddy Rankin come down with that bad ear? Martha thought nothing of it, and the next thing she knowed he got this raging fever. A pure miracle of the Lord the child didn't go deaf, they said."

Little Buddy Rankin was a seasoned waterman with two children of his own. I wondered idly what fixed memory they would have of me in twenty or thirty years.

Captain Billy's son Otis emerged from the unpainted crab shipping shed. That meant the boat was coming in. He walked to the end of the pier ready to catch the line. Those of us waiting moved out of the lee of the building to watch the ferry chug in. It was small and, even before it was close enough to reveal its peeling paint, seemed to sag in the water. Grandma was right. It was an old boat, a tired boat. My father's boat was far from new. It had belonged to another waterman before he bought it, but it was still lively and robust, like a man who's spent his life on the water. Captain Billy's ferry, though much larger, drooped like an old waiting woman. I buttoned my jacket against the wind and concentrated on Captain Billy's sons Edgar and Richard who had jumped ashore and were helping Otis tie up the ferry with graceful, practiced steps.

My father had walked up. He smiled at me and touched my arm in greeting. For a happy moment, I thought he'd spied me from his boat and had come on purpose to say hello. And then I saw his gaze turn toward the hatch of the under deck passenger cabin. It was Momma he had come to meet and Caroline, of course. Hers was the first head out of the opening, wrapped against the wind in a sky blue scarf. Just enough of her hair had escaped to make her look fresh and full like a girl in a cigarette ad.

"Hey, Daddy!" she called out as she came. "Daddy's here, Momma," she said back over her shoulder toward the cabin. Our mother's head appeared. She was having more trouble on the ladder than Caroline, for, in addition to a large purse, she was trying to negotiate a huge shopping bag.

Caroline, meantime, had skipped quickly around the narrow deck and jumped lightly to the dock. She kissed our father on his cheek, a gesture that never failed to embarrass me. Caroline was the only person I knew who kissed in public. It was simply not done on our island. At least she wouldn't try to kiss me. I was sure of that. She nodded, grinning. "Wheeze," she said. I nodded back without the smile. Daddy met Momma halfway round the deck and took the shopping bag. No unnecessary touching, but they were smiling and talking when they got off the boat.

"Oh, Louise. Thank you for bringing the wagon. They're still more groceries in the hold."

I smiled, proud of my thoughtfulness, conveniently forgetting it was Grandma who had sent me down to the dock.

Two other island women emerged from the cabin door, and then, to my surprise, a man. Men usually rode up top on the bridge with Captain Billy. But this was an old man, one whom I had never seen before. He had the strong stocky build of a waterman. His hair, under a seaman's cap, was white and thick and hung almost halfway down his neck. He had a full mustache and beard, both white, and was wearing a heavy winter overcoat, despite the fact that it was April. And he was carrying what I imagined one might call a "valise." It must have been heavy because he put it down on the dock as he waited quietly with the rest of us for Captain Billy's sons to hand up the luggage and groceries from the hold.

Momma pointed out her two boxes, which my father and I loaded precariously onto the wagon. They were too large to fit into the bed of the wagon, so we perched them slantwise, tilting down into the middle. I knew I would have to go slowly, for if I hit a bump, there were likely to be groceries all over the narrow street.

All the time I was watching the stranger out of the corner of my eye. Two more ancient bags and a small trunk were brought up and put beside him. By now everyone was staring. No one would have so much baggage unless he planned to stay for quite some time.

"Somebody meeting you?" Richard asked, not unkindly.

The old man shook his head, staring down at the luggage piled around him. He looked a little like a lost child.

"Got a place to stay?" the young man asked.

"Yes." He lifted his overcoat collar up as though to protect himself from the cold island wind and jerked his hat down almost to his bushy eyebrows.

By now the crowd upon the dock was positively leaning in his direction. The island held few secrets or surprises beyond the weather. But here was a perfectly strange man. Where had he come from, and where was he planning to stay?

I felt my mother's elbow. "Come along," she said quietly, nodding a good-bye at my father. "Grandma will be worrying."

I had seldom felt so exasperated—to have to go home in the middle of this unfolding drama. But both Caroline and I obeyed, leaving the little scene on the dock behind, making our slow progress up the narrow oyster-shell street between the picket fences that enclosed each house. The street was only wide enough for four people to walk abreast. The crushed oyster shells underfoot rattled the wagon so that I could feel the vibrations in my teeth.

There was such a scarcity of high land on Rass that for generations we had buried our dead in our front yards. So to walk down the main street was to walk between the graves of our ancestors. As a child I thought nothing of it, but when I became an adolescent, I began to read the verses on the tombstones with a certain pleasant melancholy.

Mother, are you gone forever
To a land so bright and fair?
While your children weep unstopping
Can you hear us? Do you care?

Most of them were more bravely Methodist in flavor.

God will keep you little angel
Till we greet you by and by.
For a moment is our sorrow
Joy forever in the sky.

My favorite was for a young man who had died more than a hundred years before, but to whom I had attached more than one of my romantic fantasies.

Oh, how bravely did you leave us
Sailing for a foreign shore
How our hearts did break within us
At the thought of Nevermore.

He had been only nineteen. I fancied that I would have married him, had he lived.

I needed to concentrate on the groceries. Momma still had the large shopping bag. Caroline could hardly bear to go as slowly as the two of us had to, so she tended to skip on ahead and then come back to share some of the details of her trip to the mainland. It was one of these times when she was walking toward us that she suddenly lowered her voice.

"There he is. There's that man from the ferry."

I looked back over my shoulder, being careful to keep my free hand on the grocery boxes.

"Don't be rude," Momma said.

Caroline leaned toward me. "Edgar is pulling all his stuff in a cart."

"Hush," Momma warned. "Turn around."

Caroline was slow to obey. "Who is he, Momma?"

"Shh. I don't know."

Despite his age the man was walking remarkably fast. We couldn't hurry because of the wagon, so he soon overtook us and walked purposefully down the street ahead as though he knew exactly where he was going. There was no longer any sense of a lost child in his manner. The Roberts' house was the last one on the street, but he walked right past it, to where the oyster-shell street gave way to the dirt path across the southern marsh.

"Where's he think he's going?" Caroline asked.

The only thing farther along the path besides the marsh itself was one long-since abandoned house.

"I wonder—" Momma began, but we were turning in at our own gate, and she didn't finish the sentence.

5

The stranger from the ferry offered no explanation for
his presence on the island. Gradually, the people of Rass
built one from ancient memory lavishly cemented with
rumor. The man had gone to the Wallace place, which
had been deserted for twenty years since the death of
old Captain Wallace six months after his wife. He had
found it without asking anyone the way and had moved
in and begun to put it into repair as though he belonged
there.

"He's Hiram Wallace," Grandma had announced—everyone over fifty had come to the same conclusion. "The
old ones thought he was dead. But here he is. Too late
to bring them neither comfort."

Bit by bit, straining my short patience to its utmost
limit, the story of Hiram Wallace emerged. Call's grandmother told him that when she was a child, there had
been a young waterman by that name, the only child of
Captain Charles Wesley Wallace. It was back in the days
when nearly every boat on the Bay was under sail, before
hard blue crabs brought in much money. Captain Wallace

and his son tonged for oysters in the winter, and in the summer they netted fish, chiefly menhaden and rockfish. That they had made a tidy profit was evidenced by the size of their house, which stood apart from the rest of the village. As my grandmother remembered it, their land had been large enough in those days for real grass to grow in a pasture, enough to support one of the few cows in the island's history.

What was left of the land was now all marsh, but the house, though neglected, had survived. We children had always regarded it as haunted. There were tales that Captain Wallace's ghost appeared to chase off intruders. It took me years to figure out that the purpose of the ghost story was to keep young courting couples from wandering down the path to the old Wallace place and taking advantage of the privacy.

One day I had talked Call into exploring the house with me, but just as we stepped onto the porch, a huge orange-colored tomcat came shrieking out a broken window at us. It was the only time in our lives that Call outran me. We sat gasping for breath on my front stoop. One part of my mind was saying that it had only been one of Auntie Braxton's cats. She was said to keep sixteen, and anyone who had ever been as close as her front door would have sworn by the smell that there were at least that many and more. The other part of my mind was reluctant to let it go as simply as that.

"Have you ever heard," I asked, "have you ever heard that ghosts will take an animal form when they are angry?" Now that my breath was back I let my voice glide out in a dreamy way.

Call jerked around to look me in the face. "No!" he said.

"I was reading this book," I began to improvise (of course, I'd never seen any such book). "In this book, this scientist investigated places where ghosts were supposed to be. He started out saying that there was no such thing as ghosts, but being a scientist he had to admit finally that he couldn't explain certain things any other way."

"What things?"

"Oh—" I thought fast while drawing out the syllable. "Oh—certain furry beasts that took on the personality of a dead person."

Call was clearly shaken. "What do you mean?"

"Well, for instance, suppose old Captain Wallace when he was alive didn't want any visitors."

"He didn't." Call said darkly. "My grandma told me. After Hiram left, they lived all by themselves. Never spoke to nobody hardly."

"See?"

"See what?"

"We were fixing to visit him without an invitation," I whispered. "He was yelling at us and chasing us away."

Call's eyes were the size of clam shells. "You're making that up," he said. But I could tell that he believed every word of it.

"Only one way to be sure," I said.

"How you mean?"

I leaned close and whispered again. "Go back and see what happens."

He jumped to his feet. "Suppertime!" He started out the yard.

I had done my work too well. I was never able to persuade Call to return to that old empty house with me, and somehow, I was never quite able to go there alone.

Now that the strange old man was there, the house was no longer empty, and the whole island was trying to unravel the mystery. All the old people agreed that Hiram Wallace was in his youth the hope of every island maiden's heart, but that he had left Rass with his father's money and blessing to go to college. It was an unusual enough occurrence that even someone from our island who had gone to college fifty years ago was remembered for it. People also recalled, though this point was discussed at considerable length, that he had returned home without a degree, and that he had, in some undefinable way, changed. He had never been too sociable before he left, but he was positively silent when he returned. This only made the hearts of the young girls beat the harder, and no one had suspected that anything was wrong with him until the day of the storm.

The Bay is famous for its sudden summer storms. Before they can read their school primers, watermen learn how to read the sky and to head for the safety of a cove at the first glimmer of trouble. But the Bay is wide, and sometimes safety is too far away. In the old days, the watermen would lower their sails and use them as tents to protect themselves from the rain.

This is the story that the old people told: Captain Wallace and his son, Hiram, had let down their sails and were waiting out the storm. The lightning was so bright and near that it seemed to flash through the heavy canvas of the sail, the roaring and cracking enough to wake the dead sleeping in the depths of the water. Now, a man who is not afraid at a time like this is a man without enough sense to follow the water. But to fear is one thing. To let fear grab you by the tail and swing you around is another. This, Call's grandmother said, was what Hiram Wallace had done: terrified that the lightning would strike the tall mast of his father's skipjack, he had rushed out from under his sail cover, taken an ax, and chopped the mast to the level of the deck. After the storm passed, they were sighted drifting mastless on the Bay and were towed home by an obliging neighbor. When it became apparent that the mast had been chopped down, rather than felled by lightning, Hiram Wallace became the butt of all the watermen's jokes. Not long after, he left the island for good . . .

Unless, of course, the strong old man rebuilding the Wallace house was the handsome young coward who had left nearly fifty years before. He never said he was, but then again, he never said he wasn't. Some of the islanders thought a delegation should be sent to ask the old man straight out who he was, for if he were not Hiram Wallace, what right did he have taking over the Wallace property? The delegation was never sent. April was nearly over. The one slow month of the watermen's year was coming to an end. There was a flurry of overhauling and painting and mending to be done. Crabs were moving and the men had to be ready to go after them.

"I bet he isn't Hiram Wallace," I said to Call one day in early May.

"Why not?"

"Why would a man come to Rass in the middle of a war?"

"Because he's old and has nowhere else to go."

"Oh, Call. Think. Why would a person come to the Bay right now of all times."

"Because he's old—"

"The Bay is full of warships from Norfolk."

"So? What does that have to do with Hiram Wallace?"

"Nothing. That's just it, dummy. Who would want to know about warships?"

"The navy."

"Call. Don't you get it?"

"There's nothing to get."

"Warships, Call. What better place to spy on warships than from a lonely house right by the water?"

"You read too much."

"I suppose if someone was to catch a spy they'd take him to the White House and pin medals on him."

"I never heard of kids catching spies."

"That's just it. If two kids were to catch a spy—"

"Wheeze. It's Hiram Wallace. My grandma knows."

"She *thinks* he's Hiram Wallace. That's what he wants everyone to think. So they won't suspect him."

"Suspect him of what?"

I sighed. It was obvious that he had a long way to go before he was much of a counterspy, while I was putting myself to sleep at night performing incredible feats of daring on behalf of my embattled country. The amount of medals Franklin D. Roosevelt had either hung around my neck or pinned to my front would have supplied the army with enough metal for a tank. There was a final touch with which I closed the award ceremony.

"Here, Mr. President," I would say, handing back the medal, "use this for our boys at the front."

"But, Sara Louise Bradshaw—" Franklin D. Roosevelt for all his faults never failed to call me by my full name. "But, Sara Louise Bradshaw, this medal is yours. You have earned it with your great cunning and bravery. Keep it and hand it down to your children's children."

I would smile, a slightly ironic little smile. "Do you think, Mr. President, with the life I lead, that I will live long enough to have children?" That question never failed to reduce Franklin D. Roosevelt to silence touched with awe.

In my dreams I always went it alone, but in real life it seemed selfish. Besides, I was used to doing things with Call.

"Okay, Call. First we got to work out a plan."

"A plan for what?"

"To catch this kraut in the very act of spying."

"You're not going to catch him spying."

"Why not?"

"Because he's not a spy."

What can you do with a man who has no faith? "All right. Who is he then? Just answer me that."

"Hiram Wallace."

"Good heavens."

"You're cussing again. My grandma—"

"I am not cussing. Cussing is like 'God' and 'hell' and 'damn.' "

"See!"

"Call. How about pretending? Just for fun, pretend the guy is a spy, and we've got to get the proof."

He looked uncertain. "Like one of your jokes?"

"Yes. No." Sometimes Call could be perfectly sensible and at other times you could have gotten more sense out of a six-year-old. "It's like a game, Call." I didn't wait for him to answer. "Come on." I started running for the path through the salt meadow marsh with Call puffing behind me.

If Call's family was as poor as my grandmother said they were, I could never figure out how Call got so fat. As a matter of fact, both his mother and grandmother were fat. I thought that if you were poor you were skinny. But the evidence seemed to contradict this. And Call had other problems with running besides his weight. Like all of us, his shoes came from the Sears Roebuck catalog. To order shoes from a catalog, you stood on a piece of brown wrapping paper, and your mother drew a pencil line around both your feet. These outlines were sent to the mail-order house, and they sent you shoes to fit the brown wrapping-paper feet. But the brown paper outlines didn't tell the mail-order house how fat your feet were on the top. For that reason, poor Call never had a pair of shoes that would lace properly. The tops of his feet were so fat that once he got his shoes laced up, there was nothing left to make a proper bow. So when he ran, his shoes often came unlaced and flapped up and down on his heels.

It was low tide, so I left the path and began making my way through the marsh. My plan was to give the old Wallace house a wide berth and come up on it from the south side. The old man would never expect people from that direction.

"Wait!" Call cried out. "I lost my shoe."

I went back to where Call was standing on one leg like an overweight egret. "My shoe got stuck," he said.

I pulled his shoe out of the mud for him and tried to clean it off on the cordgrass.

"My grandma will beat me," he said. It was hard for me to imagine Call's tubby little grandmother taking a switch to a large fifteen-year-old boy, but I held my peace. I had a greater problem than that. What would Franklin D. Roosevelt say about a spy who lost his shoe in the salt marsh and worried aloud that his grandma would beat him? I sighed and handed Call the shoe. He put it on and limped back to the path.

"Sit down," I commanded.

"On the ground?"

"Yes, on the ground." What did he expect, an easy chair? Then I cleaned his shoes and mine as best I could with my handkerchief. My mother had trouble persuading me to carry one because I was a lady, but I now realized that a handkerchief was an invaluable tool for a counter-spy—to erase fingerprints, and so forth. "Now," I said, "I'm going to fix your shoestrings." I unlaced his strings and started again, skipping the second and fourth holes. This way I could make the lace long enough to provide a decent bow.

"There," I said, tying them for him as though he were a little child.

"You left out four holes."

"Call. I did it on purpose. So they wouldn't come loose all the time."

"They look dumb."

"Not as dumb as you'd look in your sockfeet."

He pretended to ignore this and stared at his shoelaces, as though trying to decide whether to retie them or to leave them be.

"Why don't you think of it as a secret signal?"

"A *what*?"

"Counterspies have to have ways of identifying themselves to other counterspies. Like secret code words. Or wearing a special kind of flower. Or—tying their shoes a certain way."

"You can't make me believe that spies tie their shoestrings funny."

"Just ask Franklin D. Roosevelt when we meet him."

"That's one of your jokes."

"Oh, come on. You can tie them again later, after the mission."

He had his mouth set to argue, but I didn't wait for a retort. Good heavens. The war would be over and he'd still be sitting there fussing about his shoestrings. "Follow me and keep low."

The cordgrass was about two feet high. There was no way, short of crawling through the mud on our bellies, that we could approach the Wallace house unseen. But there is a way of feeling invisible that makes one almost believe it's true. At any rate, I felt invisible, creeping bent over toward that great gray clapboard house. My heart was beating as fast and noisily as the motor on the *Portia Sue.*

There was no sound of life from the house. Earlier I had heard sawing and pounding. Now everything was quiet except the gentle lapping of the water on the nearby shore and the occasional cry of a water bird.

I signaled for Call to follow me to the southwest corner of the house, and then, keeping close to the side, we slipped silently to the first window facing south. Carefully, I raised my head until my eyes could peer over the sill into the room. It was evidently the room that the old man had chosen for his workshop. Weather-beaten chairs, their cane bottoms sagging and broken, were arranged to serve as sawhorses. The floor was covered with wood curls and sawdust. The sounds I had heard from across the marsh came from here, but the old man was no longer in the room. I gestured Call to stay down, that there was nothing to see, but of course he stuck his head up and peered in, just as I had done.

"No one there," he said in what he mistook for a whisper.

"Shhhhh!" I waved my hand in a violent "get down," but he was in no hurry. He gazed into the room as though it were full of great art rather than pine boards and wood curls.

I gave up trying to signal him and crept ahead to the next window. Slowly, very slowly, bracing my hand against the side of the house for support, I raised my head to the level of the window—straight into a great staring glass eye. I must have screamed. At least I did something to make Call begin to run as fast as he could around the house and in the direction of the path. I didn't run—not because I wasn't terrified, not because I wouldn't have liked to run, but because my feet had lost all power of movement.

The glass eye raised itself slowly from my face and a human voice said, "There you are. I didn't mean to scare you."

I tossed my head, trying vainly to imitate the counterspy of my imagination, hoping that a clever, careless remark would float effortlessly from my lips, but my mouth was dry as sawdust and no remark, careless or otherwise, was about to emerge.

"Would you like to come in?"

I turned frantically to find Call and located him a hundred feet away on the path toward the village. He had stopped running. I felt a surge of gratitude for him. He hadn't deserted me, not really.

"Your friend, too," the old man said, putting his periscope down on a table and smiling warmly through his white beard.

I licked my mouth, but my tongue was almost as dry as my lips. Franklin D. Roosevelt was hanging the Congressional Medal of Honor around my neck, saying, "Without regard for her personal safety, she entered the very stronghold of the foe."

"Ca-all." My voice cracked wide open on the word. "Ca-all."

He started back in a sort of zombielike walk. I could feel the presence of the man in the window above me. Call came up and stood right behind me, his breath coming from his open mouth in noisy pants. We were both fixed on the form above us.

"Won't you come in and have a cup of tea, or something?" The man said invitingly. "I haven't had any visitors since I got here except for an old tomcat."

I could feel Call stiffen like a dead fish.

"He acted like the place belonged to him. I had a time convincing him otherwise."

Call butted me in the back with his stomach. I butted him back with my behind. Good heavens. Here we were on the very trail of a spy and Call was going to get upset by a ghost—a made-up ghost, one I had made up. Annoyance drove out panic.

"Thank you," I said. My voice was a little too loud and there was a distinct quaver in it, so I tried again. "Thanks. We'd like tea, wouldn't we?"

"My grandma don't allow me to drink tea."

"The boy will have milk," I said grandly and flounced around to the front door. Call followed at my heels. By the time we got around the house, the man was there, holding the door open for us. *Without regard for her personal safety . . .*

There was very little to sit on inside the house. The man pulled a rough plank bench around for Call and me, and after he'd put a kettle on a two-burner propane stove and puttered about his kitchen a bit, he came in and sat down on a homemade stool.

"Now. You are—"

I was still in the process of deciding whether or not counterspies gave their actual names in a situation like this when Call spoke up. "I'm Call and she's Wheeze."

The man began unaccountably to laugh. "Wheeze and Call," he said gleefully. "It sounds like a vaudeville act."

How rude—to sit there laughing at our names.

"It would be better if it was Wheeze and Cough. Still, Wheeze and Call is pretty good."

I sat up very straight on the bench. To my utter amazement, not to say disgust, I realized that Call was giggling. I gave him a look.

"It's a joke, Wheeze."

"How can it be a joke?" I asked. I almost said *"It's not funny,"* but I stopped myself in time. Fortunately, the kettle whistled, and the man got up to make the tea. I gave Call a glare that should have stopped the tide, but he kept on laughing. I'd never heard him laugh in my life and here he was shrieking like a gull over garbage about something that was just plain insulting.

The man handed me a mug of very black tea. "I've only got tinned milk," he said to Call while returning to the kitchen.

"That's okay," Call said, wiping the tears off his face with the back of his wrist. "Wheeze and Cough," he repeated to me. "Don't you get it?"

"Of course I get it." I was trying to figure out how I was going to get down the black stuff I had been handed. "I just don't think it's funny."

The man came back from the kitchen carrying a mug. "Not funny, eh? Oh, well, I'm out of practice." He handed the mug to Call. "It's half tinned milk and half water."

Call tasted it. "Good," he said.

I waited for him to offer me something to put in my tea, but he didn't. He just got himself a mug of the black brew and sat down.

"My real name is Sara Louise Bradshaw," I said, forgetting that minutes ago I had decided against revealing my true name.

"That's a very nice name," he said politely.

"My real name is McCall Purnell, but everybody calls me Call."

"I see," he said slyly. "If I want you, I just call Call."

"Call Call!" cried Call, as though it was the most original idea as well as the funniest thing he had ever heard. "Call Call! Did you get that, Wheeze? It's a joke."

Good heavens. "I don't suppose," I said, loading my voice with significance, "I don't suppose that you would tell us your name."

The man feigned surprise. "I thought everyone on this island knew my name."

Both Call and I leaned forward, waiting for him to say more, but he didn't. I was puzzling it out, whether to press him further or to play it casually, when Call blurted out, "You don't seem like neither spy."

The old man raised an eyebrow at me. I'm sure I turned the color of steamed crab. How do counterspies keep from blushing? He stared at me unmercifully for a minute. I was shrinking into the bench. "Why," he asked accusingly, "why aren't you drinking your tea?"

"Tin—tin—tin," I stammered.

"Rin tin tin," shrieked Call.

The man laughed, too, but at least he got up and brought the tin of milk over to me. My hands were shaking with rage or frustration or exasperation, who knew which, but I managed to fill the mug to the brim with the thick yellowish milk. He waited in front of me until I had sampled the brew. I took a scalding sip. It was too hot to know how it tasted, but I shook my head to indicate that it was fine. Halfway into the mug, I realized I should have asked for sugar, but then it seemed too late.

That was the way most of our early visits to the Captain's house went. We decided, Call and I, simply to call him "the Captain." On Rass any waterman who owned his own boat was called Captain So and So after he had passed fifty. I wouldn't call him Captain Wallace, because he'd never actually claimed the name. I kept going to see him in the fading hope that he'd turn out to be a real spy and I could have a medal after all. Call kept going because the Captain told great jokes, "not like yours, Wheeze, really good ones."

At any rate, it was Call the Captain liked, not me. If I'd been a more generous person, I'd have been happy that Call had found a man to be close to. He didn't remember his own father, and if any boy needed a father it was Call. But I was not a generous person. I couldn't afford to be. Call was my only friend. If I gave him up to the Captain, I'd have no one.

6

It is hard, even now, to describe my relationship to Caroline in those days. We slept in the same room, ate at the same table, sat for nine months out of each year in the same classroom, but none of these had made us close. How could they, when being conceived at the same time in the same womb had done nothing to bind us together? And yet, if we were not close, why did only Caroline have the power, with a single glance, to slice my flesh clear through to the bone?

I would come in from a day of progging for crab, sweating and filthy. Caroline would remark mildly that my fingernails were dirty. How could they be anything else but dirty? But instead of simply acknowledging the fact, I would fly into a wounded rage. How dare she call me dirty? How dare she try to make me feel inferior to her own pure, clear beauty? It wasn't my fingernails she was concerned with, that I was sure of. She was using my fingernails to indict my soul. Wasn't she content to be golden perfection without cutting away at me? Was she to allow me no virtue—no shard of pride or decency?

By now I was screaming. Wasn't it I who brought in the extra money that paid for her trips to Salisbury? She ought to be on her knees thanking me for all I did for her. How dare she criticize? How dare she?

Her eyes would widen. Even as I yelled, I could feel a tiny rivulet of satisfaction invading the flood of my anger. She knew I was right, and it unsettled her. But the lovely eyes would quickly narrow, the lips set. Without a word, she would turn and leave me before I was through, shutting off my torrent, so that my feelings, thus dammed, raged on in my chest. She would not fight with me. Perhaps that was the thing that made me hate her most.

Hate. That was the forbidden word. I hated my sister. I, who belonged to a religion which taught that simply to be angry with another made one liable to the judgment of God and that to hate was the equivalent of murder.

I often dreamed that Caroline was dead. Sometimes I would get word of her death—the ferry had sunk with her and my mother aboard, or more often the taxi had crashed and her lovely body had been consumed in the flames. Always there were two feelings in the dream—a wild exultation that now I was free of her and . . . terrible guilt. I once dreamed that I had killed her with my own hands. I had taken the heavy oak pole with which I guided my skiff. She had come to the shore, begging for a ride. In reply I had raised the pole and beat, beat, beat. In the dream her mouth made the shape of screaming, but no sound came out. The only sound of the dream was

my own laughter. I woke up laughing, a strange shuddering kind of laugh that turned at once into sobs.

"What's the matter, Wheeze?" I had awakened her.

"I had a bad dream," I said. "I dreamed you were
dead."

She was too sleepy to be troubled. "It was only a
dream," she said, turning her face once more to the wall
and snuggling deep under her covers.

But it was I who killed you! I wanted to scream it
out, whether to confess or frighten, I don't know. I beat
you with my pole. I'm a murderer. Like Cain. But she
was breathing quietly, no longer bothered by my dream
or by me.

Sometimes I would rage at God, at his monstrous al-
mighty injustice. But my raging always turned to remorse.
My wickedness was unforgivable, yet I begged the Lord
to have mercy on me, a sinner. Hadn't God forgiven
David who had not only committed murder, but adultery
as well? And then I would remember that David was
one of God's pets. God always found a way to let his
pets get by with murder. How about Moses? How about
Paul, holding the coats while Stephen was stoned?

I would search the Scriptures, but not for enlighten-
ment or instruction. I was looking for some tiny shred
of evidence that I was not to be eternally damned for
hating my sister. Repent and be saved! But as fast as I
would repent, resolving never again to hate, some demon
would slip into my soul, tug at the corner, and whisper,

"See the look on your mother's face as she listens to Caroline practice? Has she ever looked at you that way?" And I would know she hadn't.

Only on the water was there peace. When school let out in the middle of May, I began getting up long before dawn to go crabbing. Call went along, somewhat grudgingly, because I was unwilling to explain my great zeal for work. I had formulated a plan for escape. I was going to double my crab catch and keep half the money for myself, turning over to my mother the usual amount. My half I would save until I had enough to send myself to boarding school in Crisfield. On Smith Island to the south of us there was no high school, not even the pretense of one that we had on Rass. The state, therefore, sent any Smith Islanders who continued school after the elementary level to a boarding school in Crisfield. The prices were not out of sight. Too high, it was true, for an island family without state aid to contemplate, but low enough for me to dream and work toward. It seemed to me that if I could get off the island, I would be free from hate and guilt and damnation, even, perhaps, from God himself.

I was too clever to pin all my hopes on crabs. Crabs are fickle creatures. They always know when you need them too much and pick precisely that season to make themselves scarce. I must give the impression, therefore, despite my early risings, that I didn't much care how lucky we were. When we were on the water, poling through the eelgrass, I took pains to say at just about dawn, "This is the nicest time of day, isn't it, Call? Who cares if the crabs are here or not? Let's just relax and enjoy ourselves."

Call would give me a look that indicated that I had lost my mind, but he was smart enough not to think it out loud. I can't swear that I fooled the crabs, but our catches were good that summer. Still, I wasn't going to count too heavily on crabs. I began casting about for other ways to make money.

I found what seemed a sure thing in the back of a Captain Marvel comic book in Kellam's store. I even squandered a dime of my hard-earned cash to buy the book, which I hid with my other treasures in the underwear drawer.

WANTED: Song Lyrics
Cash for your poems!

Cash. That was a word to make the creative juices flow. The fact that most of the poetry I'd ever read came off tombstones didn't stop me. I listened to the radio, didn't I?

> *There'll be bluebirds over*
> *The white cliffs of Dover*
> *Tomorrow, just you wait and see.*
> *There'll be love and laughter*
> *And peace ever after*
> *Tomorrow, when the world is free.*

Any idiot could figure it out. Two rhyming lines, stuffed with romance, a third that neither rhymes nor makes sense right away, two more romantic ones, then the third that also rhymes with the earlier unrhymed one and sort of makes sense.

> *When the gulls fly over the Bay*
> *They cry that you're far away.*
> *But we didn't part.*
> *Though you're far across the sea,*
> *You're not far away to me,*
> *You're in my heart.*

It had all the elements—romance, sadness, an allusion to the war, and faithful love. I fancied myself the perfect lyricist—romantic, yet knowledgeable.

I tried it out on Call in the boat one day.

"What's that supposed to mean?"

"The girl's boyfriend is away at war."

"Then why are the gulls crying? Why should they care?"

"They don't really care. In poems you can't say plain out what you mean."

"Why not?"

"Then it's not poetry anymore."

"You mean a poem's supposed to lie?"

"It's not lying."

"Go on. Ain't neither gull on this Bay up there boo-hooing 'cause some sailor's gone to war. If that ain't a plain out lie, I don't know what is."

"It's a different way of talking. Makes it prettier."

"It ain't pretty to lie, Wheeze."

"Forget about the gulls. How about the rest of it?"

"The rest of what?"

"The rest of my poem, Call. How does it sound?"

"I forget."

I gritted my teeth to keep from yelling at him and then with super patience read it through again.

"I thought you's going to forget about the gulls."

"No, *you* forget them. How does the rest sound?"

"It don't make neither sense."

"What do you mean?"

"Either the guy's away or he ain't. You got to make up your mind."

"Call. It's a poem. In real life he is far away, but she thinks about him all the time, so she feels like he's real close."

"I call it dumb."

"Just wait until you fall in love."

He looked at me as though I'd proposed some indecent act.

I sighed. "Did you hear the one about the Australian who wanted to buy a new boomerang but he couldn't get rid of his old one?"

"No. What about him?"

"Get it? A boomerang. He wanted to buy a new boomerang, but he kept getting the old one back every time he threw it away."

"Why should he even want a new one? The old one's still perfectly good, isn't it?"

"Call. Just forget it."

He shook his head, the picture of patient disbelief, and I forgot I was pretending not to care about crabs and devoted my full attention to the pesky varmints. I like to recall that we netted two full baskets of rank peelers that day.

No one had told me to turn over all the money I made crabbing. I just always had. When I started, I guess, it hadn't occurred to me that it was mine to keep. We always lived so close to the edge of being poor. It made me feel proud to be able to present the family with a little something extra to hold onto. While my parents never carried on much over it, I was always thanked. When my grandmother would criticize me, I could remember, even if the laws of respect kept me silent, that I was a contributing member of the household in which she and Caroline were little more than parasites. It was a private comfort.

But no one ever said I had to turn over *every* penny I made to the stoneware pickle crock in which the household money was kept.

Why then did I feel so guilty? Wasn't it my right to keep some of my hard-won earnings? But what if Otis should say something to my father about all the crabs he was buying from us? What if Call's mother should brag to my mother about how much money Call was bringing home these days? I divided my share exactly down the middle. If there was a penny in doubt, the penny went into the crock. I was contributing almost as much as I had during the previous summer, but I wasn't taking the money proudly to Momma for her to count out and put into the crock. I was slipping it in myself and then saying later, "Oh, by the way, I left a little in the crock." And my mother would thank me quietly, just as she always had. I never said I was putting everything in. I never lied. But then no one ever asked.

If only there were some other way to make money. Call's total lack of enthusiasm for my poem had had a dampening effect. I knew perfectly well that he was as qualified to judge poetry as he was to judge jokes, which was not at all, but still, he was the only human being I could risk reading it aloud to. If only he could have said something like, "I don't know anything about poetry, but it sounds fine to me." That would have been gracious, almost honest, and would have given me a real boost when I needed it.

As it was, I waited a week or so, then pulled myself together enough to copy the poem out on clean notebook paper and mail it to Lyrics Unlimited. Even before it could have been delivered to the P.O. Box in New York, I began haunting the docks when the ferry (which also served as the mail boat) came in. I didn't have the nerve to ask Captain Billy directly if there was any mail for me, but I hoped that if I just happened to be standing there, he'd see me and let me know. I didn't know that he never opened the sack before he took it to Mrs. Kellam, who served as postmistress. But I did know that Mrs. Kellam was a noisy gossip. I dreaded the thought of her asking my grandmother about a mysterious letter arriving from New York addressed to me.

It was about that time that our day-old Baltimore *Sun* carried huge headlines about the eight German saboteurs. They had been landed by submarine on Long Island and Florida and almost immediately caught. I knew, of course I knew, that the Captain was not a spy, but as I read, it felt as though I were swallowing an icicle. Suppose he had been. Suppose Call and I had caught him and become heroes? It seemed such a near miss that suddenly it was important to me to find out more about the old man. If he was not a spy, if he was indeed Hiram Wallace, why had he come back after all these years to an island where he was hardly remembered except with contempt?

7

Call and I had been so busy crabbing since school let out that we'd hardly been to visit the Captain together. Call, I knew, usually went to see him on Sunday afternoons, but my parents liked me to stay closer by on Sundays. I didn't mind. The long sleepy afternoon was perfect for writing lyrics. By now I had nearly a shoe box full, just waiting for Lyrics Unlimited to write and demand all that I could deliver.

So Call was surprised when, on a Tuesday, I proposed that we wind up the crabbing an hour early and pay a visit to the Captain.

"I thought you didn't like him," Call said.

"Of course I like him. Why shouldn't I like him?"

"Because he tells good jokes."

"That's a stupid reason not to like somebody."

"Yeah. That's what I thought."

"What d'you mean?"

"Nothing."

I decided to ignore the implied insult. "You can learn a lot from someone who comes from the outside. Take

Mr. Rice. I guess Mr. Rice taught me more than all my other teachers put together." All two of them.

"About what?"

I blushed. "About everything—music, life. He was a great man." I talked and thought about Mr. Rice as though he were dead and gone forever. That's how far away his Texas army post seemed.

Call was quiet, watching my face. I knew he was fixing to say something but didn't quite know how to say it. "What's the matter?" I asked him. As soon as I asked, I knew. He didn't want me to visit the Captain with him. He wanted the Captain all to himself. Besides, he was suspicious of me. I decided to tackle the matter directly.

"Why don't you want me to visit the Captain?"

"I never said I didn't want you to visit the Captain."

"Well, what are we waiting for? Let's go."

He shrugged his shoulders unhappily. "Free country," he muttered. It didn't make any sense, but I knew what he meant—that if there had been a way to stop me, he would have.

The Captain was tending crab lines on his broken-down dock. I poled the boat in close before he heard us and looked up.

"Well, if it isn't Wheeze and Cough," he said, smiling widely and touching the bill of his cap.

"Wheeze and Cough, get it?" Call yelled back to me from the bow. He shook his head, smiling all over his face. "Wheeze and Cough, that's really good."

I tried to smile, but my face had too much basic integrity for me even to pretend I had heard something funny.

Call and the Captain gave each other a "don't mind her" look, and Call threw the Captain the bowline and he tied us up. I don't mind admitting I wasn't too keen to step out on that ramshackle dock, but after Call had jumped onto it, and it had only shuddered a bit, I climbed carefully out and walked off to the shore as quickly as I dared.

"I'm going to fix it." The Captain hadn't missed my anxiety. "Just so many things to do around here." He nodded at Call. "I tried to get your friend here to give me a hand, but—"

Call blushed. "You can't hammer on a Sunday," he said defensively.

Hiram Wallace would have known that. Nobody on the island worked on the Sabbath. It was as bad as drinking whiskey and close to cursing and adultery. I racked my brain for the next question—the one that would prove to Call beyond doubt that the Captain was no more Hiram Wallace than I was. "Don't you recall the Seventh Commandment?" I asked slyly.

He lifted his cap and scratched his hair underneath. "Seventh Commandment?"

I had him. That is, I almost had him. I hadn't reckoned on Call. Call who snorted and almost yelled, "Seventh? Seventh? Seventh don't have neither to do with hammering on Sunday. Seventh's the one," he stopped, suddenly embarrassed and lowered his voice, "on adultery."

75

"Adultery?" The Captain started laughing out loud. "Well, I'm too old to worry about that one. Now there was a time—" He grinned mischievously. I suspect Call wanted him to go on as much as I did, but the old man stopped right there. Like offering candy to a child and then yanking back your hand with some excuse about saving his teeth, I thought.

"Today is Tuesday," Call said as we started for the house.

"Tuesday! Then—then—" the Captain seemed terribly excited. "Then tomorrow is Wednesday, and after that comes Thursday! Friday! Saturday! Sunday! And Monday!!"

I thought Call would die laughing on the spot, but he managed to control himself enough to gasp, "Get it, Wheeze? Get it?"

If I couldn't smile at "Wheeze and Cough," how was I to force a laugh at a recitation of the days of the week?

"Don't mind her, Captain. She don't catch on too good."

"Too well." At least I could demonstrate proper grammar. "Too well."

"Too well. Too well," repeated the Captain chirpily, lifting his hand to his ear. "Hark? Do I hear the mating call of a feathered friend of the marshland?"

Call, naturally, collapsed. All I could think of was if we'd netted a spy like this, Franklin D. Roosevelt would have thrown him back. Good heavens.

Eventually, Call recovered from his hysterics enough

to explain to the Captain that since it was Tuesday and not yet suppertime, he and I would be glad to lend a hand fixing up the old dock or house or whatever else the Captain might want doing around the place. In fact, Call added, we could come at about this time *every* afternoon, except Sunday of course, and help out.

"I'd want to pay you something," the Captain said. My ears stretched practically to the top of my head, and I opened my mouth to utter a humble thanks.

"Oh, *no,*" said Call. "We couldn't think of taking money from a neighbor."

Who couldn't? But for once in his life Call talked faster than I could think, and the two of them snatched away my time and energy and sold me into slavery before I had breath to hint that I wouldn't be insulted by a small tip every now and then.

That was how we came to spend two hours every afternoon slaving for the Captain. I noticed grimly that he didn't mind at all ordering us around, even though we were supposed to be doing him a favor. We didn't have our tea break after the first week because tin was becoming scarce and the Captain was short on canned milk. And, as he explained, since he could no longer offer Call milk, it would have been mean for the two of us to stop for tea. I would have been glad to stop for any excuse, even that awful tea. When you're fourteen and your body is changing as mine was that summer, you just plain get tired, but I couldn't admit it. Both Call and the Captain seemed to regard me as mentally deficient, since I couldn't appreciate their marvelous humor. I couldn't let them make fun of me physically as well.

Nothing went right for me that summer, unless you count the fact that when my periods began, almost a year after Caroline's of course, they began on a Sunday morning *before* I left the house for church instead of after, but the stain went clear through my pants and slip to my only good dress. Momma let me pretend to be sick. What else could she do? I couldn't wash and dry my dress in time for Sunday school.

My grandmother kept saying things like "What's the matter with her? She don't look sick to me. Just don't want to worship the Lord." And "If she was mine, I'd give her a good smack on the rear. That'd perk her up fast enough."

I was terrified that Momma would betray me and tell Grandma the real reason I was staying home. But she didn't. Even Caroline tried to shush Grandma up. I don't know what Grandma told her old friends, but for weeks after that they'd all ask sweetly about my health, both physical and spiritual.

My spiritual health was about on a par with a person who's been dead three days, but I wasn't about to admit it and get prayed for out loud on Wednesday night by that bunch of old sooks.

8

I used to try to decide which was the worst month of the year. In the winter I would choose February. I had it figured out that the reason God made February short a few days was because he knew that by the time people came to the end of it they would die if they had to stand one more blasted day. December and January are cold and wet, but, somehow, that's their right. February is just plain malicious. It knows your defenses are down. Christmas is over and spring seems years away. So February sneaks in a couple of beautiful days early on, and just when you're stretching out like a cat waking up, bang! February hits you right in the stomach. And not with a lightning strike like a September hurricane, but punch after punch after punch. February is a mean bully. Nothing could be worse—except August.

There were days that August when I felt as though God had lowered a giant glass lid over the whole steaming Bay. All year we had lived in the wind, now we were cut off without a breath of air. On the water the haze was so thick it was like trying to inhale wet cotton. I began to pray for a real blow. I wanted relief that badly.

In February the weather sometimes gave us a vacation, in August, never. We just got up earlier every morning until finally we met ourselves going to bed. Call and I didn't get up quite as early as my father, who may have never gone to bed between tending to his floats and going out to crab, but we were up well before dawn, trying to sneak a fair catch of crabs from the eelgrass before the sun drove us off the water.

I had a faint hope that the Captain, not being an islander, or at least, not a regular islander, would take the heat as an excuse to slow down a bit. But Call fixed that.

"We're coming in from crabbing early these hot mornings," he blabbed. "We could come on over here and get lots more done of a day."

"I can't come before dinner," I said. "Momma expects me home to eat."

"Well, fiddle, Wheeze," Call said. "You all eat by eleven. Don't take more'n ten minutes to eat."

"We don't stuff like scavengers at our house," I said. "I couldn't possibly get here that fast. Besides, I got chores."

"We'll be here by noon," he told the Captain cheerily. I could have choked him. That meant at least four and a half hours of gut-ripping work in the heat for nothing. Nothing.

The Captain, of course, was delighted. His one concession to the temperature was that we work indoors and not on the dock in the sun. He began planning out loud all the projects the three of us could complete by the time school opened. I managed, with a lie about my mother needing me, to get away by four-fifteen. I wanted to get to the post office before supper. It would have been better perhaps if I had not, for there it was, my letter from Lyrics Unlimited. I ran with it to the tip of the island, to my driftwood stump, and sat down to open it, my hands shaking so they made a poor job of it.

Dear Miss Bandshaw:

CONGRATULATIONS!!! YOU ARE A WINNER! LYRICS UNLIMITED is delighted to inform you that your song, while not a money prize winner, is a WINNER in our latest contest.Given an appropriate musical setting, YOUR LYRICS could become a POPULAR SONG played on the radio waves all over America and even to our boys overseas. We urge you to let us set your words to music and give them this OUTSTANDING OPPORTUNITY. You might well be the lyricist of an all-time hit. You might well hear your song on the HIT PARADE. Your lyrics deserve this chance. All you need to do is send a check or money order (no stamps, please) for $25 and leave the rest to us.

81

We will

    Set YOUR WORDS to music

    Print the sheet music

    Make copies available to

      THE PEOPLE in the world

      of POPULAR MUSIC

And WHO KNOWS?! The next song to top the
HIT PARADE may be YOURS! ! ! !

    Don't lose this chance! Time is limited! Send
in your $25 today and put yourself on the ROAD
TO FAME AND FORTUNE.

                    Sincerely,

                    your friends at

                    LYRICS UNLIMITED

Even I, wanting so much to believe, could tell it was
mimeographed. The only thing typed in was my name,
and that had been misspelled. I was a fool, but I'm proud
to say, not that big a fool. Heartsick, I ripped the letter
down to its last exclamation point and flung it like confetti
out into the water.

August and February are both alike in one way. They're
both dream killers.

The next day the orange tomcat reappeared. It was
the same cat, I'm sure, that had scared Call and me that
time four years before when we had decided to investigate
the house, and the same cat that the Captain had finally
driven out after the first week or so he had lived there.

The cat marched in through the open front door as though he were the long-absent landlord popping in to check out the tenants.

The Captain was furious. "I thought I got rid of that fool thing months ago." He got his broom and took after the huge tom, who calmly jumped onto the kitchen table. When the Captain took a swing at him there, he leaped daintily to the floor, taking a cup down with his tail.

"Damn it to hell!"

I had the capacity to imagine such language, but neither Call nor I had ever really heard it spoken. I think we were as fascinated as we were shocked.

"Captain," said Call, when he recovered himself slightly, "do you know what you said?"

The Captain was still stalking the cat and answered impatiently, "Of course I know what I said. I said—"

"Captain. That's against the commandments."

He took another futile swing before he answered. "Call, I know those blasted commandments as well as you do, and there is not one word in them about how to speak to tomcats. Now stop trying to play preacher and help me catch that damn cat and let's get him out of here."

Call was too shocked now to do anything but obey. He ran out after the cat. I started laughing. For some reason, the Captain had at last said something I thought was funny. I wasn't just giggling either. I was belly laughing. He looked at me and grinned. "Nice to hear you laugh, Miss Wheeze," he said.

"You're right!" I screeched through my laughter.

"There's not—I bet there's not one word in the whole blasted Bible on how to speak to cats."

He began to laugh, too. Just sat down on the kitchen stool, the broom across his knees, and laughed. Why was it so funny? Was it because it was so wonderful to discover something on this island that was free—something unproscribed by God, Moses, or the Methodist Conference? We could talk to cats any way we pleased.

Call reappeared carrying the struggling tom. He looked first at the Captain and then at me, apparently baffled. He had never seen us laughing together, of course. Maybe he didn't know whether to be pleased or jealous.

"Who—who—" puffed out the Captain. "Who is going to take that damned animal back to Trudy Braxton?"

"Trudy Braxton!" I think both Call and I yelled it. We had never heard anyone call Auntie Braxton by her Christian name. Even my grandmother, who must have been nearly the old woman's age, called her "Auntie."

After the first shock, my feeling was one of pleasure. It really was. I no longer wanted the Captain to be a Nazi spy or an interloper. I wanted him to be Hiram Wallace, an islander who had escaped. That was far more wonderful than being a saboteur to be caught or an imposter to be exposed.

"I'll take the cat back," I said. "If the stink don't get me first."

For some reason my irreverent description of Auntie Braxton's house triggered Call. "Did you hear what she said?" he asked the Captain. " 'If the stink don't get me first.' " Then he and the Captain were laughing their heads off.

I grabbed the cat from Call just as it wriggled free. "Come along," I said, "before I call you a stinking name or two." I wasn't quite bold enough to use the forbidden curse word aloud, but I thought of it several times quite happily as I made my way up the path and to Auntie Braxton's house.

I hadn't exaggerated the smell. The windows of the house were open and the overwhelming ammonia essence of cat stood like an invisible wall between me and the front yard. The tom was scratching and struggling to get out of my grasp, leaving stinging red lines all over my bare arms. If I hadn't been afraid that he would turn and run straight back to the Captain's, I would have dropped him on the front walk and run back myself. I had, however, a duty to perform, so I marched bravely up the walk to Auntie Braxton's door.

"Auntie Braxton!" I yelled her name over unhappy cat sounds coming from the other side of the door. If I let go the tom to knock or open the door, I might lose him, so I just stood there on the dilapidated porch and hollered. "Auntie Braxton. I got your cat."

From within a cat howled in reply, but no human voice accompanied it. I called again. Still no answer from the old lady. It occurred to me that I might be able to push the cat through the torn window screen. I went over to the window. The hole was large enough if I stuffed the creature in a bit. As I stooped to do so, I saw something dark lying on the front room floor. There were cats perched on top of it and cats walking across it, so for a minute I simply stared at it, not recognizing it for what it was—a human form. When I did, I panicked. Throwing the cat down, I half tripped over it in my hurry to be gone. I raced back to the Captain's house where I nearly fell over the door stoop, panting out my terror.

"Auntie Braxton!" I said. "Lying dead on the floor with cats crawling all over her."

"Slow down," said the Captain. I tried to catch my breath and repeat myself, but after two words he was already past me and walking, almost running up the path toward the old woman's house. Call and I followed. We were both terrified, but we ran to catch up to him and stayed at his heels. No matter what terrible thing was going on, we wanted to be with him and each other.

The Captain pushed open the door. People never locked their houses on Rass. Most doors didn't even have locks. The three of us went in. No one was bothering about the smell anymore. The Captain knelt down beside the old woman, scattering cats in every direction.

Call and I hung back a little, wide-eyed and breathing fast.

"She's alive," he said. "Call, you go down to the dock. As soon as the ferry docks, Captain Billy's going to have to take her to the hospital."

Relief washed over me like a gentle surf. It wasn't that I'd never seen a dead body. On an island, you can't get away from death. But I'd never found one. Never been the first person accidentally to stumble in on death. It seemed more terrible somehow to be the first one.

"Don't just stand there, Sara Louise. Go find some men to help me carry her down to the dock."

I jumped and ran to obey. It was not until later that I realized that he had called me by my full name, Sara Louise. No one bothered, not even my mother, to call me Sara Louise, but he had done it without thinking. Strange how much that meant to me.

I got my father and two other men from their crab houses, and we raced back to Auntie Braxton's. The Captain had found a cot mattress, and he and my father gently rolled the old woman over and lifted her to the mattress. The Captain covered her with a cotton blanket. I was glad, for her thin legs seemed indecent somehow poking out from her faded housedress. Then the four men began to lift the awkward makeshift stretcher. As they did so, the old lady moaned, like someone disturbed by a bad dream.

"It's all right, Trudy, it's me, Hiram," the Captain said. "I'll take care of you." My father and the other two men gave one another funny looks, but no one said anything. They had to get her to the hospital.

9

"Trudy" was what did it. Simply by using Auntie Braxton's first name, the Captain confirmed himself as the true Hiram Wallace. He still didn't go to meet the ferry in the afternoon like most folks, or hang around Kellam's after supper matching water stories, or go to church. But despite these aberrations he seemed to be accepted as an islander, simply because he had called Auntie Braxton "Trudy," a name nobody had used for her since she was a young woman.

Call's life and mine took a strange turn at that time. The Captain decided that while Auntie Braxton was in the hospital, the three of us should tackle her house. I tried weakly to argue that it was like trespassing to clean up someone's house without her permission, and trespassing was something Methodists were forever bent on getting forgiveness for, so it was likely to be a fairly serious sin. The Captain just snorted impolitely at that. If we didn't do it, he said, the Ladies' Society of the Methodist Church was likely to take it on as a good deed. Although

Auntie Braxton went regularly to church, she had, for years, been considered strange, and once her cat population had passed four or five, she had been on very strained terms with the other women of Rass.

"Would Trudy rather have them poking about her property than us?"

"She'd rather have nobody, I bet."

He sadly admitted that I was right, but since the alternative to our doing the cleaning was having it become a missionary endeavor, I had to agree that we were certainly the lesser of two evils.

The problem, of course, was the cats. Until something could be done about them, there was no hope of getting the house in any kind of order.

"How in the world did she feed them?" I asked. It had always seemed to me that Auntie Braxton was below even Call's family on the poverty scale.

"The wonder is she didn't feed them better," the Captain said. "These poor things look half-starved."

"Cat food costs a lot of money," I said, trying to remember if Auntie Braxton had ever been known to buy fish from a local waterman to feed to her cats. Anyone else would have used scraps, but anyone else would have had more people than cats in the house.

"I would have thought Trudy had more money than most people on the island," the Captain said.

Even Call was flabbergasted. "What makes you think a thing like that?" he asked. We both remembered that

Auntie Braxton got a basket from the Ladies' Society at Thanksgiving and Christmas. Not even Call's family rated a basket.

"I was here when her father died," the Captain said, as though the two of us should have known such a simple fact as that. "Old Captain Braxton had plenty, but he never let on. He let his wife and child scrimp by on next to nothing. Trudy found the money after they both died. And it scared her something silly to suddenly find all this cash, so she come running to my mother. My mother treated her like she was her own daughter. Poor Momma," he shook his head, "she never gave up hoping I'd marry Trudy. Well, anyway, Momma told her to put it in a bank, but I doubt that Trudy did. What did she know about mainland banks? What's left of it after all these years is probably hidden right here in this house, if the damn cats haven't chewed it up."

"Maybe it ran out," I said. "It's been a long time."

"Maybe. It was a lot of money." He suddenly looked at us both, changing his tone abruptly. "Look," he said, "don't say anything about any money. If she'd have wanted anyone else to know about it, she would have told them. I'm not even supposed to know. Just my mother."

Call and I nodded solemnly. Real intrigue was far more delicious than the pretend kind. The fact that there might be money hidden convinced me beyond a doubt that the Ladies' Society must not take over the housecleaning.

But the distasteful problem of the cats remained. The

Captain made both me and Call sit down in his clean, refurbished living room. He served me tea and Call some of his precious tinned milk, and then, very gently, he tried to explain to us what he believed had to be done.

"The only way to resolve the problem of the cats," he said, "is to dispose of them humanely."

Either I was a little slow or the language was too elegant, because I was nodding my head in respectful agreement when, suddenly, it hit me what he meant.

"You mean shoot them?"

"No. I think that would be hard to do. Besides it would make a mess and bring the neighbors running. I think the best method—"

"Kill them? You mean kill them all?"

"They're almost starving now, Sara Louise. They'll die slowly with no one to care for them."

"I'll take care of them," I said fiercely. "I'll feed them until Auntie Braxton gets back." Even as I heard myself say it, the words hacked at my stomach. All my crab money, my boarding school money—to feed a pack of yowling, stinking cats. I hated cats.

"Sara Louise," the Captain said kindly, "even if you had the money to feed them, we can't leave them in the house. They're a health hazard."

"A person's got the right to choose their own hazards."

"Maybe so. But not when it's getting to be a problem for the whole community."

"Thou shalt not kill!" I said stubbornly, remembering at the same time that only the day before I had been rejoicing that not one word of the blasted Bible applied to cats. He was gracious enough not to remind me.

"What are you fixing to do with 'em, Captain?" Call asked, his voice cracking in the middle of his question.

The Captain sighed, polishing his mug with the back of his thumb. Without lifting his eyes, he said softly, "Take them couple miles out and leave them."

"Drown them?" I was getting hysterical. "Just take them out and throw them in?"

"I don't like the idea, either," he said.

"We could take them to the mainland," I said. "They have places there like orphanages for animals. I read about it in the *Sun.*"

"The SPCA," he said. "Yes, in Baltimore—or Washington. But even there, they'd just have to put these creatures to sleep."

"Put them to sleep?"

"Kill them as gently as possible," he explained. "Even there they can't take care of everyone's unwanted cats on and on."

I tried not to believe him. How could anything that called itself the "Society for the Prevention of Cruelty to Animals" engage in wholesale murder? But even if I was right, Baltimore and Washington were too far away to do Auntie Braxton's cats any good.

"I'll borrow a boat," he said. "One that will get us out fast. You two round up the cats." He started out the door and up the path. In a moment he was back. "There's three gunnysacks on the back porch," he said.

"You'll need something to put the cats in." Then he was gone again.

Call got off the bench. "C'mon," he said. "We can't catch neither cat sitting here on our bottoms all day."

I shuddered and got up reluctantly. It would be better not to think, I told myself. If you could hold your nose to avoid a stink, or close your eyes to cut out a sight, why not shut off your brain to avoid a thought? Thus, the catching of the cats became a sport with no consequences. We took turns, one holding the bag while the other dodged about the furniture and up the stairs in pursuit. They were amazingly lively despite their half-starved appearance, and once seized and thrown into the sack, they went after one another with ungodly shrieks. Five were in the first bag—they proved to be the hardest to get—and the bag was tied tightly with cord I found in the kitchen drawer.

By the second bag, I had become more wily. In addition to the cord, I had found some cans of tuna and sardines in the kitchen. I divided a can of sardines between the two remaining gunnysacks and then smeared the oil on my hands. I risked being eaten alive, but it worked. I lured those fool cats right to me and into those infernal sacks. We got them all, all that is but the orange tom, which was nowhere in the house. Neither Call nor I had the heart to track him down. Besides, sixteen snarling cats were more than enough.

I sneaked down to our house and got the wagon. Very gingerly we loaded the live sacks onto it. We were already scratched and bitten enough. Those claws could reach through the burlap as though it weren't there. Once one of the sacks writhed and wiggled its way off the wagon and into the street, but we got it back on and down the path to the Captain's dock. He sat there waiting for us in a skiff with an outboard. He was wearing a black tie and his old blue seaman's suit. I had the feeling he was dressed for a funeral.

Without a word, Call and I put the sacks into the bottom of the boat and climbed in after them. The cats must have exhausted themselves fighting, for the sacks lay almost quiet at our feet. The Captain yanked the starter cord two or three times and the motor finally coughed and then hummed. Slowly he turned the bow and headed for open water.

It was midafternoon and the heat closed in on us unmercifully. I was aware of the smells of cat and the awful spoiled sardine smell of my own hands. I jerked them off my lap.

Just then, a piteous little cry rose from the sack nearest my feet. It sounded more like a baby than a cat, which is why, I suppose, it suddenly tore the blinders from my mind. "Stop!" I screamed, standing up in the boat.

The Captain cut the motor abruptly, telling me to sit down. But as soon as the motor died, I jumped over the washboard and swam with all my might for shore. I could dimly hear the Captain and Call yelling after me, but I never stopped swimming or running until I was home.

"Wheeze. What happened?" Caroline jumped up from the piano at the sight of me, hair streaming, clothes dripping all over the floor. I stomped past her and my mother, who had come to the kitchen door, up the stairs to our bedroom and slammed the door. I didn't want to see anyone, but of all people in the world, Caroline was the last one I wanted to talk to. I still smelled of sardines, for goodness' sake.

She opened the door a crack and slid through, leaning on it to shut it gently behind her. There was no way, now, to get down to the kitchen and wash.

"Can't you see I'm dressing?" I turned my back to the door.

"Want me to get you a towel?"

"Don't bother."

She slid out the door and came back carrying a towel. "You're a mess," she said pleasantly.

"Oh, shut up."

"What happened to you?"

"None of your business."

She got that hurt look in her great blue eyes that always made me want to smack her. She didn't say anything, just put the towel down on her bed and climbed up and sat down cross-legged beside it, dropping her shoes neatly to the floor.

"You and Call didn't go swimming, did you?"

No one was supposed to know that Call and I sometimes went swimming together.

I tried to run my fingers through my wet knotted hair.

She slipped off her bed and came over carrying the towel. "Want me to rub your hair?"

My first impulse was to shake her off, but she was trying to be kind. Even I could tell that. And I was feeling so awful that the kindness broke down all my usual defenses. I began to cry.

She got my bathrobe for me, and then she dried my hair with those powerful fingers of hers as gently as she might coax a nocturne from our old piano. So although she never seemed to urge me to talk, I began to do so, until, finally, I was pouring out my anguish, not for the cats, but for myself as murderer. It didn't matter that I had not actually thrown them into the Bay. I had cleverly lured them to their death. That was enough.

"Poor Wheeze," she said quietly. "Poor old cats."

At last I stopped crying, dressed, and combed my hair.

"Where are you going?" she asked. It was none of her business, but she had been too nice for me to say so.

"Auntie Braxton's," I said. "We have to get it cleaned up before the Ladies' Society makes it a missionary project."

"Can I come?"

"Why would you want to come? It's a filthy stinking mess."

She shrugged, blushing a little. "I don't know," she said. "Nothing better to do."

We borrowed a bucket and mop and a bottle of disinfectant as well as a pile of rags from my mother, whose face was set in a question she did not ask. As we entered Auntie Braxton's house, I watched Caroline closely. I suppose I wanted to see some sign of weakness. "Smells terrible," she said cheerfully.

"Yeah," I said, a bit disappointed that she hadn't at least gagged.

We had hardly filled the bucket with water when Call and the Captain appeared at the front door. They just stood there, hanging back a little, like a pair of naughty kids.

"Well," I said. "Back so soon."

The Captain shook his head sadly. "We couldn't do it."

Call looked as though he were about to cry. "They sounded just like little babies," he said.

I'm sure I should have felt joy and relief. Actually, what I felt was annoyance. I had spent a lot of guilt and grief over the death of those dratted cats. They had no right to be alive. "Well," I said, the dried salt was making my skin itch and adding to my irritation, "what are you going to do with them, then? We can't keep them here. You said so yourself."

Wearily, the Captain sat down in Auntie Braxton's easy chair right on top of the pile of rags I'd left there. He scrunched around under himself and fished them out. "I don't know," he was saying. "I just don't know."

"We can give them away." It was Caroline, taking over the problem just as though someone had asked her to.

"What do you mean, 'we'?" I was furious at her.

"I—you," she said. "What I mean is, just give the cats to as many people as will take them—"

"Nobody is going to take these cats," I said. "They're wild as bobcats and half-starved to boot. Nobody in their right mind would take a cat like that."

The Captain sighed his agreement. Call nodded his Methodist preacher nod. "They're wild as bobcats," he repeated. Not that any of us had ever seen a bobcat.

"So?" Caroline was undaunted. "We tame them."

"Tame them?" I snorted. "Why don't you just teach a crab to play the piano?"

"Not permanently," she said. "Just long enough to get them new homes."

"How, Caroline?" Call was definitely interested.

She grinned. "Paregoric," she said.

Call went to his house to fetch the family bottle, and I went to our house and got ours. Meantime, Caroline had prepared an assortment of sixteen saucers, cups, and bowls, rationing out the cans of tuna fish to each container. She laced each liberally with paregoric. We set them all around the kitchen floor and then brought in the gunnysacks and untied them.

Lured by the smell of food, the cats came staggering out of the bag. At first there was a bit of snarling and shoving, but since there were plenty of dishes for all, each cat eventually found a place for itself and set itself to cleaning away every trace of the drugged feast set before it.

In the end, it was as much Caroline's charm as the paregoric that worked. She took one cat to each house along the street, leaving Call and me to mind the sacks, slightly out of sight. Nobody on Rass would dare slam a door in Caroline's face. And no matter how determined the housewife might be against taking in a cat, Caroline's melodiously sweet voice would remind her that it was no small thing to save a life—a life precious to God if not to man—and then she would hold out a cat who was so doped up with paregoric that it was practically smiling. Some of them even managed a cuddly, kittenish mew. "See," Caroline would say, "he likes you already."

When the last cat was placed, we went back to Auntie Braxton's. The Captain had put chairs on top of tables and was beginning to mop the floor with hot water and disinfectant. Call told him the whole story of Caroline's feat, house by house, cat by cat. They laughed and imitated the befuddled women at the door. Caroline threw in imitations of the happy, drunken cats while the Captain and Call hooted with delight, and I felt as I always did when someone told the story of my birth.

10

The blow that I had been praying for struck the next week. While not as severe as the storm of '33, which became a legend before its waters receded, the storm of '42 is the one I will never forget.

During the war, weather was classified information, but on Rass we didn't need a city man on a radio to warn us of bad weather. My father, like any true waterman, could smell the storm coming up, even before the ominous rust-colored sunset. He had made his boat fast and boarded up the windows of our house. There was not much he could do about the peelers in our floats, except hope the storm would leave him a few of the floats and spare his crab shanty for one more season.

It is a mysterious thing how cheerful people become in the face of disaster. My father whistled as he boarded up the windows, and my mother from time to time would call to him happily out the back door. She obviously was enjoying the unusual pleasure of having him home on a weekday morning. Tomorrow they might be ruined or dead, today they had each other. And then there are things you can do to prepare for a hurricane. It is not like a thunderstorm on the water or sudden illness before which you are helpless.

Just before noon Call came by and asked if Caroline or I was going down to the Captain's.

"Sure," said Caroline cheerfully. "Soon as we finish carrying the canning upstairs." High water had more than once washed through our downstairs, and my mother didn't want to take a chance on having the fruits and vegetables she had bought on the mainland and put up for the winter dashed to the floor or swept away. "You coming, Wheeze?"

Who did she think she was, inviting me to go see the Captain? As if she owned both him and Call. Call, who had always belonged to me because nobody else besides his mother and grandmother would have him, and the Captain, who finally through all our troubles and misunderstandings had become mine as well. Now, because of one afternoon of giving away a batch of drugged cats, she thought she could snatch them both for herself. I muttered something angry but unintelligible.

"What's the matter, Wheeze?" she asked. "Don't you think we ought to help the Captain get ready for the storm?"

There she was, trying to make me look bad in front of Call. Her voice had its usual sweet tone, and her face was all concern. I wanted to smack it. "Go on down," I said to Call. "We'll get there when we can."

Later the four of us boarded up the Captain's windows.

Call, Caroline, and the Captain were calling back and forth cheerfully while we worked. The Captain didn't want to move anything to the second floor, and he laughed away my fear that the water might rise higher than his front stoop. We carried our hammers and nails and boards up to Auntie Braxton's and started on her windows. Before long my father joined us, and with his help, the work was quickly done.

"Want to spend the night at our place, Hiram?" my father asked.

The Captain smiled quickly as though thanking my father for calling him by name. "No," he said. "But I thank you. Any port in a storm, they say, but I take home port if I got a choice."

"It's going to blow mean tonight."

"I wouldn't be surprised." But the Captain gathered his tools, waved, and headed for home.

I was a sound sleeper in those days and it was my father, not the wind that woke me up.

"Louise."

"What? What?" I sat up in bed.

"Shh," he said. "No need to wake your sister."

"What is it?"

"The wind's come up right smart. I'm going to go down and take off my motor and sink the boat."

I knew that to be an extreme measure. "Want me to help?"

"No, there'll be plenty of men down there."

"Okay," I said and turned over to sleep again. He

shook me gently. "I think you better go down and get the Captain. Bring him up here in case it gets worse."

I was fully awake now. My father was worried. I jumped up and pulled on my work overalls over my nightgown. The house was shuddering like Captain Billy's ferry.

"Is it raining yet?" I asked my father at the front door. The wind was so loud that it was hard to tell.

"Soon," he said, handing me the largest flashlight. "Better wear your slicker. Now you take care and be quick."

I nodded. "You, too, Daddy."

The blow came up faster than even my father had guessed. Every now and then I would grab the paling of one of the picket fences lining the street to steady myself against the wind. It was blowing from the northwest, so making my way southeast toward the Captain's house, I had the feeling that at any moment the wind might lift me off my feet and deposit me in the Bay. When I reached the last house, where the narrow street turned into a path across the marsh, I went down on my hands and knees, shoved my slicker up out of the way, and crawled. The wind seemed too powerful now to tempt with my upright body.

If our house had been shaking, protected as it was in the middle of the village, imagine the Captain's, hanging there alone so near the water. The beam of my flashlight caught for a frightening moment the waters of the Bay, which the wind had whipped into a fury. *And everyone that heareth these sayings of mine and doeth them not, shall be likened unto a foolish man, which built his house upon the sand: And the rain descended and the floods came, and the winds blew, and beat upon that house . . .*

I began to cry out the Captain's name. How he heard me over the roar of the wind, I don't know, but he was out on the porch before I reached the house.

"Sara Louise? Where are you?"

I stood up, bracing my body as best I could against the wind. "Hurry!" I yelled. "You got to come to our house."

He came quickly, put his body in front of mine, and pulled my arms about his waist. He took my flashlight so I could grasp my hands together in front of him. "Hold tight!"

Even with his stocky waterman's body to break the wind, our journey back up the path was a treacherous one. The rain was coming down now like machine-gun fire, and the water from the marsh began to swirl up around our feet. The Captain cried out something to me, but his voice was lost in the moaning of the wind. Like all the rest of me, my hands were wet. Once they slipped apart. The Captain caught my left arm and held on tightly. Even when we got to the first picket fence, he held on. The pain in my arm became the only real thing, a sharp point of comfort in the midst of a nightmare. In the narrow street the dark houses of the village gave us some shelter from the wind, but the water of the Bay was already washing across the crushed oyster shells.

My father was not home when the Captain and I got

there. The electricity was out. My mother, white-faced in the light from the kerosene lamp, was at the stove getting coffee. Grandma was rocking back and forth in her chair, her eyes squinched shut. "Oh, Lord," she was praying out loud. "Why don't you come down and still the wind and waves? Oh, Jesus, you told the storm on Galilee, 'Peace, be still,' and it obeyed your word. Ohhh, Lord, come down now and quiet this evil wind."

As if in defiance, the moan of the wind shifted into a shriek. We were all so startled that it took us several seconds to realize that my father had come in the front door and was now pushing the old food safe against it. The door was leeward, but we all knew that later the wind would shift. We had to be ready.

"Best douse the lamp, Susan," my father said. "And the stove. Things get banging around down here and we'll have a first-class fire."

Momma handed him a cup of coffee before she obeyed.

"Now," he said. "Best be getting upstairs." He had to shout to be heard but the words were as calm as someone telling the time. "Come along, Momma," he called to Grandma. "Can't have you floating away on your rocker." He waved his flashlight toward the staircase.

Grandma had stopped her litany. Or else the wind had swallowed it. She went to the steps and began to climb slowly. My father nudged me to follow. "Oh, my blessed," Grandma was saying as she climbed. "Oh, my blessed. I do hate the water."

Caroline slept on. Caroline would probably have slept

through the Last Trumpet. I started toward her bed to wake her up. Daddy called me from the hallway. "No," he said. "Let her sleep."

I came back to where he was. "She'll miss the whole hurricane."

"Yeah. Probably will," he said. "Better get off those wet things, now. Then you should try to get some sleep yourself."

"I couldn't sleep through this. I wouldn't want to."

Even through the shriek of the wind, I could hear his chuckle. "Nope," he said. "Probably wouldn't."

When I had changed out of my wet things and cleaned myself off as best I could, I went into my parents' room. Daddy had gone down and fetched Grandma's chair so she could rock and moan as was her custom. Somehow, the Captain had changed from his wet clothes into my father's bathrobe, which barely met at his middle. Daddy and Momma were perched on the side of their bed, and the Captain sat on the edge of the only other chair. They had lit a candle in the room, which flickered because of the wind coming through the chinks of the house. Momma patted the bed beside her. I went and sat down. I wanted to snuggle up on her lap like a toddler, but I was fourteen, so I sat as close to her body as I dared.

We gave up trying to talk. It was too hard to fight the wind screaming like a giant wounded dove. We could no longer hear the sounds of Grandma's prayers or the rain or the water.

Suddenly there was silence. "What happened?" Though as soon as I asked, I knew. It was the eye. We were in the quiet eye of the storm. Daddy got up, took the flashlight, and went to the stairs. The Captain rose, pulled the bathrobe together, and followed him. I started to get up, too, but Momma put her arm across my lap.

"You can't tell how long it will last," she said. "Just let the men go."

I wanted to object, but I was tired. It wouldn't have mattered. The men were back almost before they started.

"Well, Sue, there's two foot of Bay water sloshing about down there." Daddy sat down beside her. "I'm feared it'll make a mess of your nice parlor."

She patted his knee. "As long as we're all safe," she said.

"Ohhhh, Lord," Grandma cried out. "Why must the righteous suffer?"

"We're all safe, Momma," my father said. "We're all safe. Nobody's suffering."

She began to cry then, bawling out like a frightened child. My parents looked at each other in consternation. I was angry. What right had she, a grown woman, who had lived through many storms, to carry on like that?

Then the Captain got up and went to kneel beside her chair. "It's all right, Louise," he said, as though he were indeed talking to a child. "A storm's a fearsome thing." When he said that I remembered the tale I'd heard about him cutting down his father's mast. Was it

107

possible that a man so calm had once been so terrified? "Would you like me to read to you?" he asked. "While it's still quiet?"

She didn't answer. But he got up and, taking the Bible from the bedside table, pulled his chair in close to the candle. As he was flipping through for the place, Grandma looked up. "T'ain't fitting a heathen should read the Word of God," she said.

"Hush, Momma!" I had never heard my father speak so sharply to her before. But she did hush, and the Captain began to read.

"God is our refuge and strength, a very present help in trouble." He read well, better than the preacher, almost as well as Mr. Rice. "Therefore we will not fear, though the earth be removed, and though the mountains be carried into the midst of the sea; Though the waters thereof roar and be troubled, though the mountains shake with the swelling thereof . . ."

Into my mind came a wonderful and terrible picture of great forested mountains, shaken by a giant hand that scooped them up, finally, and flung them into the boiling sea. I had never seen a mountain, except in a geography text. I was fourteen, and I had never even seen a real mountain. I was going to, though. I was not going to end up like my Grandma, fearful and shriveled.

They told me later that I finally slept through the worst part of the hurricane. When the eye passed, the wind came up from the south even more fiercely than before. "Grabbed this old house by the scruff of the neck and shook the bejeebers out of it," my father said. "But I couldn't wake you for nothing. Snoring away like an old dog."

"I didn't snore!" I was horrified at the thought of the Captain watching me while I snored.

"Snored so loud, you plumb drowned the wind." He was teasing me. At least I hoped my father was teasing.

It was not one of those hurricanes like the one that was to hit the Atlantic Coast in '44, not one of those hurricanes that go down in books. No island lives were lost in the storm of '42. No human lives, at any rate. The storm did accomplish without conscience what we had been too fainthearted to do. It reduced the island's cat population by at least two-thirds.

11

It was the bluest, clearest day of the summer. Every breath of air was delicious with just enough of a clean, salt edge to wake up all your senses. If the Captain and I had just stood on the porch with our eyes closed, it would have been a perfect day. For while our noses and lungs feasted on nature's goodness, our eyes were assaulted by evidence of her savagery.

The water had left our living room, but it was still in the yard, level with the porch. Riding the muddy surface were sections of picket fence, giant tree limbs, crab pots, remnants of floats and crab houses, boats, and . . . "What's that?" I had grabbed the Captain's arm.

"A coffin," he said matter of factly. "These storms will dig them up sometimes. Just replant them is all." His mind was clearly not on the dead. "Look here," he said. "There's no safe walking to my place this morning. We'd best go back in and give your mother a hand."

The thought of our sodden, muck-filled downstairs dragged at me like a lead weight on a crab pot. "Don't you want to see what happened to your house?" I asked.

This was a day for adventure, not drudgery.

"Plenty of time to see later when the water's down," he said, turning to go back inside.

"My boat!" That was it. We could pole the skiff down to his house, maneuvering around the debris as we would ice floes. He cocked his head. I'm sure he doubted that my stubby little skiff could have survived the storm.

At first we couldn't tell. The gut had disappeared under the foot of water flooding the yard, bringing with it the same floating dump heap we had seen swirling about the front yard. The day before, my father had tied the boat, not just to the pine to which I usually secured her bow line; he had run lines from her stern to the fig tree on one side and the cedar on the other. The three trees were still there, looking a bit like little boys after their summer haircuts, but still there. From the porch I could, at last, make out the three now taut lines, and then I caught sight of her washboards just above the water line.

"She's here!" I was half off the porch when the Captain grabbed me.

"You want lockjaw or typhoid or a combination?" He indicated my bare legs and feet.

I was too happy to be offended. "Okay," I said. "Just a minute." He waited until I fetched my father's old boots. He had worn his good ones when he left earlier to see about his own boat and the crab shanty.

We bailed out the skiff until it was bobbing merrily on the surface. The Captain loosed the lines on the house side of the still invisible gut, and then I climbed into the boat, pulled myself along the rope to the cedar tree, and loosed that knot as well. The Captain fetched the pole from the kitchen, and after he had handed it in to me in the stern, he climbed in and sat down facing me, his arms tightly folded across his chest.

He let me maneuver the skiff through the wreckage of the flood without even peeking over his shoulder to see what I might be about to hit. I poled us along what I thought might be the line of the gut. The water was too murky and trash-filled to tell. Usually my pole was only a foot or so in the water, but then suddenly it would go down three feet and I knew I had found the gut again.

The Captain looked so somber, I could almost imagine I was an Egyptian slave taking Pharaoh on a tour of the flooded Nile Delta. In fifth-grade history we had spent a lot of time worrying about the flooded river deltas of the ancient world. I would be one of those wise slaves who could read and write and dare to advise their masters. Now, for example, I would be reassuring the Pharaoh that the flood was a gift from the gods, that once it receded, the rich black earth of the delta would bring forth abundant grain. Our storehouses would be full to overflowing even as they had been when the great Joseph had been the Pharaoh's minister.

My reverie was punctured by a raucous cackling and complaining from a tiny house floating past us. "Hey!" I said. "That looks like the Lewises' chicken coop." The live occupants of the coop were squawking their unhappiness to the world as they traveled along.

The storm had been capricious. Some roofs were gone, while the next door house was not only intact but the fence and shed as well. In some yards people were already trying to collect things and clean up the debris lodged against their fences. I called out to them and waved.

They waved back and shouted greetings like, "Hey there, Wheeze. Y'all make out all right?"

And I'd answer, "Yessir. Least the house is all right." Seldom had I felt such warmth from my island neighbors. I nodded and waved and smiled. I loved everyone that morning.

I was well past and around the last house on the village street when I realized that I had lost my bearings. I should be over the marsh now. The sun was starboard, so I should have been heading straight for the Captain's house.

I made a funny squeak in my throat that startled the Captain. "What is it?" He jerked around to see what I was staring at.

I was staring at nothing. Nothing. Not a tree, not a board. Nothing was left at the spot where the Captain's house had stood the night before.

It took us both a few minutes to take it in. I circled the spot in the boat, or tried to. My pole was going down too deep for me to dare venture out too far. There was nothing to tell us if we were over the south marsh or the place where the Wallace house had stood. It was all Bay now.

At first I could do nothing but stare at the muddy water. Finally, I stole a look at the Captain. His eyes looked glazed, and he was pulling at the hair of his beard with the fingers of his left hand. He realized that I was watching him and cleared his throat.

"We used to have cows," he said. "Did you know that?"

"I heard it. Yes."

"Though the earth be removed," he was mumbling. "Though the mountains be carried into the midst of the sea."

I wanted to say how sorry I felt, but it seemed childish. I hadn't even lost my boat pole. He had lost everything.

He crossed his arms once more even more tightly across his chest. Squinting his eyes, he said in a rough voice, "Well. That's that."

As I turned the boat, I tried to read his meaning. At last I said, "Where do you want to go?"

His laugh came out something like a snort. I shipped the pole and sat down on the thwart opposite him. "I'm really sorry," I said.

He shook his head as though to shake off my concern, his eyes glittering. His hands dropped to his lap. He was wearing clothes borrowed from my father, an old blue workshirt and denim pants that were a little too tight for him. He seemed to be watching his right thumb rub the knuckles of his left hand. For all his white beard, he looked like a little boy trying not to cry. I was terrified that I might actually see tears in his eyes and so to avoid that sight more than anything else, I slipped off the thwart, crossed the narrow space between us on my knees, and put my arms around him. The rough shirt scraped my chin, and I was aware of the pressure of his knees against my stomach.

Then, suddenly, something happened. I can't explain it. I had not put my arms around another person since I was tiny. It may have been the unaccustomed closeness, I don't know. I had only meant to comfort him, but as I smelled his sweat and felt the spring of his beard against my cheek, an alarm began to clang inside my body. I went hot all over, and I could hear my heart banging to be let out of my chest. "Let go, stupid," part of me was saying, while another voice I hardly recognized was urging me to hold him tighter.

I pulled back abruptly and, putting the thwart between us, grabbed up the hard, solid pole, stood and jammed it down into the water. I didn't dare speak, much less look at him. What must he think of me? I knew that anything that made a person feel the way I felt at that moment had to be a deadly sin. But I was less concerned at the moment with God's judgment than the Captain's. Suppose he laughed? Suppose he told someone? Call or, God forbid, Caroline?

I dared a glance at his hands. The fingers of his right hand were nervously tapping his knee. I had never noticed how long his fingers were. His nails were large, rounded at the bottom and blunt and neat at the tips. He had the cleanest fingernails of any man I'd ever seen—it was the male hand in the ad reaching to put the diamond on the Ponds-caressed female hand. Why had I never noticed before how beautiful his hands were? I wanted to hold one in both of my hands and kiss the fingertips. Oh, my blessed, I was going crazy. Just looking at his hands was doing the same wild things to the secret places of my body that holding him had done.

I poled faster and tried to keep my eyes and mind totally on getting the boat back to the house. I kept banging into debris. I was sure he could tell how agitated I was. I kept waiting for him to say something. Anything.

"Well," he said. My heart went straight through my ribs at the sound. "Well." A short explosive sigh. "That's that."

That's what? something inside my head was crying. I rammed the boat into the back porch, leaped out, and secured the line on a post. Then, without looking back, I raced into the house up into the sanctuary of my bedroom.

"What's the matter, Wheeze?" No sanctuary. No hiding place. Caroline was there to question me as I dived onto my bed and buried my head under the pillow. "For goodness' sake, Wheeze? What on earth is going on?"

When I refused to answer, she finished dressing and went downstairs. I could hear voices, muffled as they were by the pillow. I waited for laughter. Slowly, as I calmed, I knew that the Captain would never tell my mother or my grandmother what had happened in the boat. Call and Caroline, perhaps, but not the others.

But even if he never told a soul, how was I to face him again? Just thinking of his smell, his feel, his hands, made my body go hot all over. "He's older than your grandmother," I kept saying to myself. "When your grandmother was a child, he was nearly a man already." My grandmother was sixty-three. She seemed like a hundred, but she was sixty-three. I knew because my father had been born when she was sixteen. The Captain had to be seventy or more. I was fourteen, for mercy's sake. Fourteen from seventy was fifty-six. *Fifty-six*. But then my mind would go to the curve of his perfect thumbnail, and my body would flame up like pine pitch.

I heard my father come in the front door. I jumped off the bed and tried to compose myself before our small streaky mirror. I could not pretend I had not heard him, and no one would understand any excuse for my not coming down to hear his report. I would have to be stretched out dead to remain upstairs. I ran a comb through my wild hair and banged down the steps. Everyone turned at the racket. I just caught the Captain's face. He was smiling. I'm sure I flushed all over, but no one, after that first glance, was taking notice of me. They wanted to find out what was happening at the harbor.

"The boat's all right." That was the first and only really vital thing we needed to know.

"Thank the Lord," Momma said quietly, but with a force that surprised me.

"There's plenty," Daddy went on, "that aren't so lucky. A lot of the boats not sunk are all tore up. It'll be a hard year for many." Our crab house was gone and the floats as well, but we had our boat. "The dock's tore up right smart, but folks got their homes."

"Not the Captain." Caroline said it so quickly and loudly that no one else had a chance. It didn't seem right to me that the Captain should be robbed of the chance to tell his own tragedy. He had nothing else to call his own. He should have at least had his story. But Caroline was like that, snatching other people's rights without even thinking.

"Oh, my blessed," said my father. "And here I was thinking how lucky we were. Is it clean gone?"

The Captain nodded, tightening his arms across his chest as he had earlier. "Even the fast land where she stood," he said. We were all quiet. My grandmother ceased her eternal rocking for a time. At last he said, "That whole marsh was a meadow back when I was a boy. We used to keep cows." It bothered me intensely that he should be repeating the information about the cows. I couldn't understand why it meant so much to him.

"Well," my father said. "Well." He went over to the table and sat down heavily on a chair. "You best stay with us for a while."

The Captain opened his mouth to protest, but Grandma beat him to it. "Ain't neither room for another body in this house," she said. She was right, but I wanted to kill her for saying it. Just the look on the Captain's face ripped my heart right out of my chest.

"The girls can double up for a few days, Mother," my father said. "And you can have the other bed up there."

She opened her mouth wide, but he shushed her with a look. "Louise'll help you carry up a few things now."

"I couldn't think of putting you to trouble," the Captain said. The tone was a meek, broken one I'd never heard before.

"It's no trouble," I said loudly before my grandmother could interfere again. I rushed into her room and cleared her drawers in a few swoops and carried her things upstairs on a run. Half of me was bursting with joy at the thought of having him so close, the other half was in mortal terror. I seemed to have no control over myself, I who had always prided myself on keeping the deepest parts of me hidden from view. I dumped my own things into a bag and pushed it under Caroline's bed, and then as neatly as I could, folded Grandma's things and put them in my drawers. I was shaking all over. Grandma had come thumping up the stairs. She was in a rage.

"I can't think what your daddy's up to," she said, still panting from her rush up the stairs. "Letting that heathen into our house. Into my bed. Oh, my blessed. Into my very bed."

"Stop it!" I didn't say it loudly, but I said it into her face. It may have scared her. She sniffed and backed up. She climbed up on my bed. Naturally, she assumed that I would be the one to give up a bed. "I'm resting," she said. "If anybody cares."

I slammed the drawer shut and went back downstairs. How dare she hurt his feelings? He had lost everything he had in this world. I saw his beautiful hands lovingly

119

sanding the back of one of his old chairs. He had worked so hard on that house. We all had. He and Call and I. Not Caroline. It didn't belong to her, just to the three of us. But when I got to the living room, there was Caroline, giving him a cup of coffee, practically falling all over him while she did so. Then she got herself a cup and sat down beside him, her beautiful eyes mooning with pity.

"Would you like some coffee, Louise?"

"No," I said sharply. "Somebody's got to remember this is no picnic." There was no place to run to, no tip of the marsh where I could sit alone on a stump of driftwood and watch the water. I wanted to cry and scream and throw things. Instead, under almost perfect control, I got a broom and began savagely to attack the sand that was stuck like cement in the corner of the living room.

12

For the three days that the Captain lived with us, I avoided looking him in the eye. I was, instead, obsessed with his hands. They were always moving because he was intent on paying his way by helping to clean the house. By the time the water had left the yard and street, most of our downstairs, though smelling more like a crab shanty than a proper house, was at least cleaned out. We carried the stuffed chair and the couch to the front porch to let them air as best we could. Grandma's high bed had escaped the water but still smelled damp, so we put the mattress on the porch roof to sun.

The Captain treated me as though nothing had happened between us. At least I think he did. My brain was so feverish, it couldn't have judged what was natural and what was not. He called me "Sara Louise," but he had done that for some time, hadn't he? Why then did his voice speaking my name seem so heartbreakingly sweet? Tears would start in my eyes at the sound.

The second afternoon after the water was gone, he left the house for several hours. I wanted to go with him, but I couldn't trust myself. What insane thing might I do, finding myself suddenly alone with him? But after he was gone I began to worry. Would he do something foolish now that he had lost everything? I had one horrible vision of him walking straight out into the Bay until he was swallowed up. Oh, if only I could tell him that he had me—that I would never desert him. But I couldn't. I knew I couldn't.

I forgot my work and began to watch for him. Caroline and I were supposed to be putting fresh paper on the lower kitchen cabinet shelves, so that the canned goods could be brought down once more from upstairs and put away.

"Wheeze, what on earth are you doing? You've been to the front door five times in the last five minutes."

"Oh, leave me alone."

"I know what she's doing." Grandma was rocking as usual in the living room. "She's peeking around for that heathen Captain of hers."

Caroline burst into a giggle and then tried to cover it up with fake coughing. Once we were both in the kitchen and out of sight, she rolled her eyes at me and twirled her finger at her temple to indicate that she thought our grandmother was nuts.

"Yep. Yep." The voice continued from the other room. "Can't keep her eyes off that wicked man. I see it. 'Deed I do."

Caroline began to giggle in earnest then. I didn't know which one I wanted to kill more.

"I told Susan no good would come of letting that man into the house. Like letting the devil himself march in. Don't take much to bedevil a foolish girl, but still—"

My throat choked up like a swamp pond listening to her drone on and on.

"But still, they that lets the devil in cannot count themselves blameless."

I was holding a jar of string beans in my hand, and I swear, if my mother had not happened down the stairs at that moment, I might have hurled that quart at the old woman's nodding head. I don't know what my mother heard, if anything, but I suppose she sensed the hatred, the air was so thick with it. At any rate, she gently pried my grandmother from the rocker and helped her upstairs for her afternoon nap.

When she came back to the kitchen, Caroline was practically dancing across the linoleum, simply bursting to tattle. "You know what Grandma said?"

I turned on her like a red-bellied water snake. "Shut your mouth, you fool!"

Caroline blanched, then recovered. "Whosoever shall say, 'Thou fool,' shall be in danger of hell fire," she quoted piously.

"Oh, my blessed," said Momma. She didn't often resort to such a typical island expression. "Is the world so short on trouble that you two crave to make more?"

I opened my mouth but shut it again hard. *Momma, I wanted to cry out, tell me I'm not in danger of hell fire.* My childhood nightmares of damnation were rising fast, but there was no place for me to run. How could I share with my mother the wildness of my body or the desperation of my mind?

As I finished putting away the canned goods in frozen silence, my own hands caught my eye. The nails were broken and none too clean, the cuticles ragged. There was a crack of red at the edge of my index finger where a hangnail had been chewed away.

"She's lovely, she's engaged, she uses Ponds" the advertisement read, showing two exquisitely white hands with perfectly formed and manicured nails, long nails, and a diamond ring sparkling on the gracefully curved left hand. A man with strong clean hands would never look at me in love. No man would. At the moment, it seemed worse than being forsaken by God.

The five of us were already at the supper table when the Captain got back. He knocked formally at the door. I jumped and ran to the screen to open it, even though my mother had not indicated that I must. He was standing there, his blue eyes sagging with tiredness, but with a warm smile parting his lips above the beard. In his arms he was carrying the huge orange tomcat.

"Look what found me," he said, as I opened the door.

Caroline came running. "You found the old orange cat!" she cried, just as though she had had some relation to the creature. She reached out for it. I was almost glad because I figured the tom would go wild at her touch. But it didn't. The storm must have broken its spirit, for it lay purring close to Caroline's chest. "You sweet old thing," she murmured, rubbing her nose in its fur. If Caroline had been relegated to the devil, she probably would have tamed him as well. She gave the cat some of our supper fish in a bowl and set it on the kitchen floor. The cat plunged its head blissfully into the bowl.

The Captain followed Caroline to the kitchen and rinsed his hands by pouring a scant dipper of our precious fresh water over them. Then he took out a large white handkerchief and wiped them carefully before he came back into the living room to sit down at the table. I concentrated on keeping my eyes off his hands, knowing now that they were more dangerous for me than his face, but sometimes I couldn't help myself.

"Well," he said, as though someone had asked him, "I hitched a ride to Crisfield today."

Everyone looked up and mumbled, though it was evident that he was going to tell us what he had been up to whether or not we prodded.

"I went to see Trudy in the hospital," he said. "She has that perfectly good house standing there empty. It occurred to me she might not mind my staying there until I can work out something more permanent." He carefully unfolded his large cloth napkin and lay it across his lap, then looked up as though awaiting our judgment.

My grandmother was the first to speak. "I knowed it," she muttered darkly without a hint of what it was she knew.

"Hiram," my father said, "no need for you to rush away. We're proud to have you with us."

The Captain flicked a glance at Grandma, who had her mouth open, but before she got her words past her teeth, he said, "You're mighty gracious. All of you. But I could be cleaning out her place while I live there. Make it fit for her to come home to. It would be a help to both of us."

He left right after supper. He had nothing to move, so he simply walked out with the orange tom at his heels.

"Wait," called Caroline. "Wheeze and I will walk you over." She grabbed her light blue scarf and tied it loosely about her hair. She always looked like a girl in an advertisement when she wore that scarf. "Come on," she said, as I hung back.

So I went with them, my legs so heavy that I could hardly lift them. It's better, I tried to tell myself. As long as he is here I will be in danger. Even if I do not give myself away, Grandma will see to it. But, oh, my blessed, did I hate to see him go.

School opened, and I suppose that helped. With Mr. Rice gone, there was only one teacher for the whole high school. Our high school, which had about twenty students at full strength, was down now to fifteen since two had graduated the previous spring and three had gone off to war. Six of us, including Call and Caroline and me, were freshmen, five were sophomores, three juniors, and a lone senior girl, Myrna Dolman, who wore thick glasses and doggedly maintained the ambition she had harbored since first grade to become a primary schoolteacher. Our teacher, Miss Hazel Marks, used to hold Myrna up to the rest of us as an example. Apparently, the ideal pupil in Miss Hazel's eyes was one who wrote neatly and never smiled.

I wasn't smiling much that fall, but my handwriting didn't improve a whit thereby. Without Mr. Rice, all the fun of school was gone. Although he had not been our teacher when we were in the eighth grade, we had been allowed every day to join the high school for music since the chorus could not do without Caroline. Even having to acknowledge that debt could not diminish my delight in our hour of music. Now, however, there was nothing to look forward to.

On the other hand, there was a certain safety in the unrelenting boredom of each day. I heard once that there are people who commit crimes with the sole purpose of being caught and put in jail. I rather understand that mentality. There are times when prison must seem a haven.

The ninth grade was seated in the worst possible place in the classroom, at the front, and to the right, away from the window. I spent hours gazing into the disapproving face of George Washington as painted by Gilbert Stuart. This experience left me with the conclusion that our first president, besides having frizzy hair, a large red hooked nose, and apple cheeks, had a prissy, even old-ladyish mouth and a double chin. All of these would have rendered him harmless, except that he also had staring blue eyes, eyes that could read everything that was going on underneath my forehead.

"Really, Sara Louise," he seemed to say everytime he caught my eye.

My mental project that fall was a study of all the hands of the classroom. It was my current theory that hands were the most revealing part of the human body—far more significant than eyes. For example, if all you were shown of Caroline's body were her hands, you would know at once that she was an artistic person. Her fingers were as long and gracefully shaped as those on the disembodied hands in the Ponds ad. Her nails were filed in a perfect arc, just beyond the tip of her finger. If the nails are too long, you can't take the person seriously, too short, she has problems. Hers were exactly the right length to show that she was naturally gifted and had a strength of will to do something about it.

In contrast I observed that Call's hands were wide with short fingers, the nails bitten well below the quick. They were red and rough to show he worked hard, but not muscled enough to give them any dignity. Reluctantly, I concluded that they were the hands of a good-hearted but second-rate person. After all, Call had always been my best friend, but, I said to myself, one must face facts however unpleasant.

Then there were my hands. But I've already spoken of them. I decided one day in the middle of an algebraic equation to change my luckless life by changing my hands.

Using some of my precious crab money, I went to Kellam's and bought a bottle of Jergens Lotion, emery boards, orange sticks, cuticle remover, even a bottle of fingernail polish, which though colorless seemed a daring purchase.

Every morning as soon as there was enough light to see by without turning on the lamp, I'd work on my hands. It was a ritual as serious as the morning prayers of a missionary, and one which I took pains to finish well before Caroline could be expected to wake up. I carefully stashed my equipment at the very back of my bottom drawer in the bureau we shared.

Despite all my cunning, I came in one afternoon to find her generously slathering her hands with my Jergens.

"Where did you get that?"

"From your drawer," she said innocently. "I didn't think you'd mind."

"Well, I do mind," I said. "You have no right to go poking around my drawers, stealing my stuff."

"Oh, Wheeze," she said, placidly helping herself to more lotion. "Don't be selfish."

"Okay," I screamed, "take it! Take it! Take everything I own!" I picked up the bottle and hurled it at the wall above her bed. It smashed there and fell, leaving a mixture of shattered glass and lotion to ooze down the wall after it.

"Wheeze," she said quietly, looking first at the wall and then at me, "have you gone crazy?"

I fled the house and was headed for the south marsh before I remembered it was no longer there. I stood shaking at the spot where the head of the old marsh path had begun, and through my tears, I thought I could just make out across the water a tiny tump of fast land, my old refuge now cut off from the rest of the island, orphaned and alone.

13

Caroline kept the Jergens Lotion incident to herself, so no one else suspected that I was going crazy. I kept the knowledge locked within myself, taking it out from time to time to admire in secret. I was quite sure I was crazy, and it was amazing that as soon as I admitted it, I became quite calm. There was nothing I could do about it. I seemed relatively harmless. After all, I hadn't thrown the lotion bottle at anyone, just the wall. There was no need to warn or disturb my parents. I could probably live out my life on the island in my own quiet, crazy way, much as Auntie Braxton always had. No one paid much attention to her, and if it hadn't been for the cats, she would have probably lived and died in our midst, mostly forgotten by the rest of us. Caroline was sure to leave the island, so the house would be mine after my grandmother and my parents died. (With only a slight chill I contemplated the death of my parents.) I could crab like a man if I chose. Crazy people who are judged to be harmless are allowed an enormous amount of freedom ordinary people are denied. Thus as long as I left everyone alone, I could do as I pleased. Thinking about myself as a crazy, independent old woman made me feel almost happy.

So since no one knew about me, the crisis demanding the family's attention centered around Auntie Braxton. She was going to be released from the hospital, which meant that the Captain would soon be homeless again.

To my father it was perfectly simple. We were the Captain's friends, we would take him in. But my grandmother was adamant. "I'll not have that heathen in my house, much less in my bed. That's what he craves. To get in my bed with me in it."

"Mother Bradshaw!" Momma was genuinely shocked. My father glanced nervously at Caroline and me. She was on the verge of laughing. I was numb with rage.

"Oh, you just think when a woman gets old no man is going to look at her that way again."

"Mother," my father said. His intenseness made her pause. "The girls—" He nodded at us.

"Oh, she's the one stirred him up," Grandma said. "She thinks he craves her, but I know. I know who he's really after. 'Deed I do."

My father turned to Caroline and me and spoke quietly. "Go to your room," he said. "She's old. You got to make allowances."

We knew we had to obey, and for once I was eager to. Caroline hung back, but I grabbed her arm and started for the staircase. I couldn't help what my parents heard, but I didn't want Caroline to hear. It was she who knew that I, not Grandma, was the crazy one.

As soon as our door was shut Caroline burst out laughing. "Can you imagine?" She shook her head. "What do you suppose is going on in that head of hers?"

"She's old," I said fiercely. "She's not responsible."

"She's not that old. She's younger than the Captain and he's not the least bit crazy." She didn't even look up to see how I was reacting. "Well," she continued in a chatty tone of voice. "At least we know he can't stay here. I can't imagine what she'd do if we invited him in again." She pulled her legs up and sat cross-legged on her bed facing toward mine. I was lying on my stomach with my head on my hands. I turned my face toward the pillow, trying not to betray myself any more than I had already. "I don't see why he can't just keep on living at Auntie Braxton's," she said.

"Because they're not married," I said. If I weren't more careful my voice alone would give me away. I cleared my throat and said as steadily as I could, "People who are not married do not live together."

She laughed. "It's not as if they'd want to do anything. My gosh, they're both too old to bother with that."

I was so hot all over at the suggestion of the Captain doing something that I could hardly breathe.

"Well?" Obviously she wanted some comment from me.

"It doesn't matter," I muttered. "It's how it looks. People don't think it looks right for people who aren't married to live together in the same house."

"Well, if people are going to be that way, they should just get married."

"What?" I swung my legs over the side of the bed and sat bolt upright.

"Sure," she said calmly, as though she were explaining a math problem. "What difference would it make? They should just get married and shut everybody up."

"Suppose he doesn't want to marry a crazy old woman?"

"He doesn't have to do anything, silly. They'd just—"

"Will you shut up about *doing* things? You have got the filthiest mind. All you can think about is *doing* things."

"Wheeze. I was talking about *not* doing anything. It would be a marriage of convenience."

"That's not the same." I'd read more than she had and knew about these things.

"Well, a marriage in name only." She grinned at me. "Like that better?"

"No. It's terrible. It's peculiar. And don't you even suggest it. It will make him think we're peculiar, too."

"It will not. He knows us better than that."

"If you mention it to him, I'll kill you."

She shrugged me off. "You will not. Honestly, Wheeze, what's got into you?"

"Nothing. It's just that he might want to marry someone else. How would it be if we made him marry Auntie Braxton and then later on, too late, he finds he's really in love with someone else?"

134

"What on earth have you been reading, Wheeze? In the first place, if you don't count Grandma who's really nuts, and Widow Johnson who still worships the image of her sainted captain, and Call's grandma, who's too fat, there is no one else. In the second place, we can't *make* him do anything. He's a grown man."

"Well, I think it's filthy even to suggest it."

She stood up, choosing to ignore my comment. At the door she listened for what might be going on downstairs and then, apparently satisfied that all was quiet, turned to me. "Come on," she said. "If you want to."

I jumped off my bed. "Where do you think you're going?"

"I'm going to get Call."

"Why?" I knew why.

"The three of us are going to see the Captain."

"Please stop it, Caroline. It's none of your business. You hardly even know him." I was trying to force my voice to remain calm with the result that all the unreleased shrieks were clogging my throat.

"I do know him, Wheeze. And I care about what happens to him."

"Why? Why do you always try to take over everybody else's life?" I thought I might strangle on the words.

She gave me her look which indicated that once again I had lost all sense of proportion. "Oh, Wheeze" was all she said.

It was up to Call to stop her. He would, I was sure— he and his tight little sense of propriety. But once she'd explained to him what a marriage "in name only" consisted of, he blushed and said, "Why not?"

Why not? I followed them to Auntie Braxton's house like a beaten hunting pup. Why not? Because, I yearned to say, people aren't animals. Because it is none of our business. Because, oh, my blessed, I love him and cannot bear the thought of losing him to a crazy old woman, even in name only.

The Captain was making tea and cooking potatoes for his supper when we arrived. He was uncommonly cheerful for a man who was about to be cast out on his ear for the second time straight. He offered to share his supper, but there was hardly enough for one person, so we all politely refused, insisting that he go ahead—at least, Caroline and Call were insisting. I was sitting tight-lipped on the other side of the room, but when Caroline and Call started to sit down at the kitchen table with him I dragged myself across the living room and dumped myself into the empty chair. As little as I wanted to be a part of the coming scene, I didn't want to be left out of it either.

Caroline waited until he had generously salted and peppered his potatoes, then she laid her elbows on the table and propelled herself a bit closer to it and thus to him. "We heard that Auntie Braxton is going to be back in a couple of days," she said.

"That's right," he said, taking a large bite of potato.

"We've been worried about where you're going to live."

He raised his hand to stop her talking and held it there until he had chewed and swallowed the bite. "I know what you're going to say, and I thank you, but I just can't."

See? See? I was smiling inside and out.

Caroline was not. "How do you know what I'm going to say?"

"You're going to ask me back to your house—and I'm grateful, but you know I can't come in on you again."

Caroline laughed. "Oh, I've got a much better idea than that."

All my smiles had dried up.

"Have you now, Miss Caroline?" He was spearing another piece of potato with his fork.

"I sure do." She leaned toward him with the kind of smile you see a woman give a man when she's got something more than politeness on her mind. "I'm proposing that you marry Miss Trudy Braxton."

"Marry?" he asked, putting down his fork and staring wide-eyed into her face. "You're suggesting that Trudy and I get married?"

"Don't worry," Call began earnestly, "you wouldn't have to—" at which point my bare heel slammed down on his bare toes. He stopped talking to give me a look of hurt surprise.

Caroline ignored us both. "Think of it this way," she said in her most sophisticated tone of voice. "She needs someone to take care of her and her house, and you need

a house to live in. It would be a marriage of convenience."
I noticed she didn't say "in name only." At least she
had a whiff of delicacy.

"I be damned," he said under his breath, looking from
one face to another. I pretended to study a torn cuticle
to miss his scrutiny. "You kids do beat the limit. Who
would have ever thought?"

"Once you get used to the idea, it'll make a lot of
sense to you," Caroline said. "It's not," she added quickly,
"that you couldn't find someplace else. Plenty of folks
would take you in. But no one else *needs* you. Not like
Auntie Braxton." She turned to me, then to Call for support.

By now I was biting away at the offending cuticle,
but out of the corner of my eye I could see Call nodding
his head vigorously, pumping up for a big affirmative
statement. "It'll make sense," he repeated Caroline's
theme. "It'll make plenty of sense, once you get used
to it."

"It will, will it?" The Captain was shaking his head
and grinning. "You sound like my poor old mother."
Eventually he picked up his fork and, using one side of
it, thoughtfully scraped the pepper off one of the potatoes.
"People," he said at last, no shadow of a grin remaining,
"people would say I did it for the money."

"What money?" Caroline asked.

"Nobody but you ever heard tell of no money," Call
said. "Me and Wheeze are the only ones you told. And
now Caroline."

"I wouldn't take a cent of her money, you know."

"Of course you wouldn't," Caroline said. What did she know?

"There probably isn't any," I said huffily. "We cleaned good and we never saw any."

He smiled appreciatively at me as though I had helped him. "Well," he said grinning. "It's a crazy idea." Something about the way he said it made me feel cold all over.

"You're going to think about it," Caroline said, rather than asked.

He shrugged. "Sure," he said. "No harm thinking crazy."

The next day he caught the ferry to Crisfield. He never even told us he was going. We had to get the word from Captain Billy. And he didn't come home that night or the next. We knew because we met the ferry each evening.

On the third day there he was, waving to us from the deck. My heart jumped to see him, and my body felt all over again how it was to be crushed against the rough material of his clothes, his heart beating straight through my backbone. Call and Caroline were waving back and calling out to him, but I was standing there shivering, my arms crossed, my hands hooked up under my arms and pressed against my breasts.

The boat was tied up, and now he was calling us by name. He wanted Caroline and me to see to something

139

in the hold and Call to come aboard and give him a hand.

Caroline, as usual, moved faster than I. "Come, look here!" she yelled. When I got to where Captain Billy's sons were handing up the freight, I saw the chair. It was huge and dark brown with a wicker seat and back and large metal wheels rimmed in hard black rubber. It took both Edgar and Richard to lift it up onto the pier. Caroline was grinning all over. "I bet he's done it," she said.

Whatever was in my look made her correct herself. "I mean," she said with an impatient sigh, "I just mean, I bet he's gone and married her."

I had no place to run to, and even if I had, it was too late. They were already emerging from the cabin. Very slowly up the ladder, first Call's head, his neck bent. Then at last the three of them, the Captain and Call carrying Auntie Braxton on a hand sling between them, she with an arm about each's shoulder. When the three of them turned around at the top of the ladder, I could see that she was wearing on her shoulder a huge chrysanthemum corsage.

"He did marry her." Caroline said it softly, but it was exploding like shrapnel inside my stomach. She ran for the wheelchair and pushed it to the end of the gangplank as proud as though she were rolling out the red carpet for royalty. Call and the Captain carefully lowered the old woman into the chair.

As he straightened up, the Captain saw me hanging

back and called to me. "Sara Louise," he said. "Come on over. I want you to shake hands with Miz Wallace here."

The old woman looked up at him when he said that, as worshipful as a repentant sinner testifying in church. When I came close, she put out her hand. Shaking her hand was like holding a bunch of twigs, but her eyes were clear and steady. I think she said, "How are you, Sara Louise?" The words were hard to decipher.

"Welcome home, Miss Trudy," I muttered. I couldn't for the life of me call her by his name.

14

I suppose if alcohol had been available to me that November, I would have become a drunk. As it was, the only thing I could lose my miserable self in was books. We didn't have many. I know that now. I have been to libraries on the mainland, and I know that between my home and the school there was very little. But I had all of Shakespeare and Walter Scott and Dickens and Fenimore Cooper. Every night I pulled the black air raid curtains to and read on and on, huddled close to our bedroom lamp. Can you imagine the effect of *The Last of the Mohicans* on a girl like me? It was not the selfless Cora, but Uncas and Uncas alone whom I adored. Uncas, standing ready to die before the Delaware, when an enemy warrior tears off his hunting shirt revealing the bright blue tortoise tattooed on Uncas's breast.

Oh, to have a bright blue tortoise—something that proclaimed my uniqueness to the world. But I was not the last of the Mohicans or the only of anything. I was Caroline Bradshaw's twin sister.

I cannot explain why, seeing how the storm had affected

our family's finances, I never told anyone that I had almost fifty dollars hidden away. Among the first things that had to be given up were Caroline's mainland voice and piano lessons. Even on generous scholarships, the transportation was too much for our slender resources. I suppose it is to Caroline's credit that she seldom sulked about this deprivation. She continued to practice regularly with the hope that spring would mark the end of a successful oyster season and give us the margin we needed to continue her trips to Salisbury. I might say to my own credit, as I needed every bit of credit available in those days, that I did not rejoice over Caroline's misfortune. I never hated the music. In fact, I took pride in it. But though it occurred to me to offer the money I had saved to help her continue her lessons, I was never quite able to admit that I had put it away. Besides, it was not that much money—and it was mine. I had earned it.

I went once to see the Captain after he got married. He invited the three of us—Caroline, Call, and me—to dinner. I suppose he meant it for a celebration. At any rate, he pulled out a small bottle of wine and offered us some. Call and I were shocked and refused. Caroline took some with a great deal of giggling about what would happen if anyone found out he had smuggled spirits onto our very dry little island. I was annoyed. The absence of alcohol on Rass (we never counted Momma's sherry bottle as real alcohol) was a matter of religious, not civil, law. We didn't even have a policeman, and there certainly was nothing resembling jail. If people had known about the Captain's wine, they would have simply condemned him as a heathen and prayed over him on Wednesday night. They'd been doing that ever since he arrived.

"I used to buy this kind of wine in Paris," the Captain explained. "It's been hard to get since the war." I assumed, of course, that he meant the war of the moment. Thinking back, I guess he must have meant World War I. I had a hard time keeping in mind how old he was.

With Auntie Braxton, there was no question. She sat at the head of the table in her wooden and wicker wheelchair, smiling a lopsided, almost simple smile. Her hair was white and so thin you could see the pink of her skull shining through. I suppose the strange angle of her smile was the result of the stroke, which is what had caused her to fall and break her hip. She tried to hold her glass in the tiny claw of her hand, but the Captain was there to hold it steady at her mouth. She took a sip, a bit of which dribbled down her chin. She seemed not to mind, keeping her clear, childlike eyes devoted to his face.

He patted her chin with a napkin. "My dear," he was saying. "Did I ever tell you about the time I had to drive a car across the city of Paris?"

For those of us who had lived all our lives on Rass, an automobile was almost more exotic than Paris. It irritated me that the Captain had never thought to tell, or chosen to tell Call and me about this adventure. For it was an adventure, the way the Captain told it.

Settling back in his own chair, he explained that he

had driven a car only once before in his life, and that on a country road in America, when his companion, a French seaman, suggested that they buy a car someone was hawking on the dock at Le Havre and take it into Paris. The Frenchman felt that it would be a wonderful way to pick up some girls, and the Captain, his pockets full of francs and with a week's shore leave in which to spend them, saw the car as a means to independence and excitement. He did not know until after the purchase was made that his companion had never driven a car before.

" 'But no matter,' " the Captain imitated the Frenchman. " 'Is easy.' " With difficulty, the Captain persuaded his friend to let him drive and then began their hair-raising trip from Le Havre to Paris, culminating in a cross-city ride at the busiest time of the afternoon.

"And then I came to a huge intersection—carts and automobiles and trucks coming at me from what seemed to be eight directions. If I stayed still I would be plowed under but to go forward was suicide."

"What did you do?" Call asked.

"Well—I shifted into first gear, grabbed the wheel as tight as I could with one hand, squeezed the horn with the other, jammed down on the accelerator with both feet, shut my eyes, and zoomed across."

"What?" cried Call. "Didn't you kill yourself?"

A peculiar noise, more like a chicken cackle than anything else, came from the end of the table. We all turned. Auntie Braxton was laughing. The others all began to laugh then, even Call, who knew the joke was at his expense. Everyone began to laugh but me.

"Don't you get it, Wheeze?" Call asked. "If he'd of killed himself—"

"Of course I get it, stupid. I just don't happen to think it's funny."

Caroline turned to Auntie Braxton and said, "Don't mind her." She flashed a beautiful smile at Call. "Wheeze doesn't think anything's funny."

"I do, too. You liar! All you do is lie, lie, lie."

She gave me her most pained expression. "Wheeze," she said.

"Don't call me Wheeze! I'm a person, not a disease symptom." It would have sounded more impressive if my voice hadn't cracked in the middle of the word *disease*.

Caroline laughed. She acted as though she thought I had meant to be funny. When she laughed, Call laughed. They looked at each other and hooted with pleasure as though something enormously witty had been said. I propped my forehead on my elbowed hand and steeled myself for the cackle from Auntie Braxton and the laugh, which reminded me of an exuberant tuba, that would come from the Captain. They didn't come. Instead, I felt a scratchy arm about my shoulder and a face close to my ear.

"Sara Louise," he was saying gently. "What's wrong, my dear?"

God have mercy. Didn't he know that I could stand anything except his kindness? I pushed back my chair, nearly knocking him down as I did so, and fled from that terrible house.

I never saw Auntie Braxton again, until she was laid out for her funeral. Caroline reported to me regularly how happy both the old woman and the Captain were. She and Call visited them almost every day. The Captain always asked Caroline to sing for them because "Trudy loves music so." He seemed to know a lot about this old woman that most people who had lived all their lives on the island didn't.

"She can talk, you know," Caroline said to me. "Sometimes you can't understand, but he always seems to. And whenever I sing she listens, really listens. Not with half her mind somewhere else. The Captain's right. She loves it. I never saw anyone who loved music so much, not even Momma." When she would say things like this, I'd just bury myself more deeply in my book and pretend I hadn't heard.

On the anniversary of Pearl Harbor, Auntie Braxton suffered a massive stroke and was rushed to the hospital by ferry in the middle of the night. She was dead by Christmas.

There was a funeral service for her in the church. It seemed ironic. Neither she nor the Captain had been to church for as long as anyone could remember, but the preacher in those days was young and earnest and gave her what was warmly regarded as a "right purty service." The Captain wanted our family to sit with him in the front pew, so we did, even Grandma who, I'm glad to say, behaved herself. The Captain sat between Caroline and me. While the congregation recited the Twenty-third Psalm—"Yea, though I walk through the valley of the shadow of death, I shall fear no evil; for thou art with me . . ." Caroline reached over and took his hand as though he were a small child in need of guidance and protection. He reached up with his free hand and wiped his eyes. And, sitting closer to him than I had in months, I realized with a sudden coldness how very old he was and felt the tears start in my own eyes.

Afterward my mother asked the Captain to come home and have supper with us, but when he refused, no one pressed him to change his mind. Caroline and Call and I walked him to the door of what was now his house. No one said a word along the way, and when he nodded to us at the door, we just nodded back and headed home. As it turned out, it was a good thing he had not come home with us. Grandma went on one of her worst rampages to date.

"He killed her, you know."

We all gaped in astonishment. Even from Grandma this was strong stuff.

"He wanted her house. I knew soon as he moved in there this was bound to happen."

"Mother," my father said quietly. "Don't, Mother."

"I reckon you want to know how he did it."

"Mother—"

"Poisoned her. That's how." She gazed about the table

in triumph. "Rat poison." She took a large bite of food and chewed it noisily. The rest of us had stopped eating entirely.

"Louise knows," she said in a sneaky little voice. She smiled at me. "But you wouldn't tell, would you? And I know why." She broke into a child's singsong jeer. "Nah nah nah nah *nah nah.*"

"Shut up!" It was Caroline who yelled what I could not.

"Caroline!" both our parents said.

Caroline's face was red with rage, but she pinched her lips together.

Grandma continued unperturbed. "Ever see how she looks at him?"

"Mother."

"She thinks I'm only a foolish old woman. But I know. 'Deed I do." She stared at me full in the eyes. I was too afraid to look away. "Maybe you helped. Did you, Louise? Did you help him?" Her eyes were glittering.

"Girls," my father was almost whispering. "Go to your room."

This time both of us obeyed immediately. Even behind the safety of our door we could not speak. There were no more jokes or excuses to be made for the silly, grumpy old woman we'd known from birth. The shock was so enormous that I found my own puny fear of exposure melting into a much larger darker terror that seemed to have no boundaries.

149

"Who knows?" the voice from *The Shadow* asks. "Who knows what evil lurks in the hearts of men?" Now we knew.

Much later, when we were getting ready for bed, Caroline said, "I've got to get away from here before she runs me nuts."

You? I thought but did not say. You? What harm can she possibly do you? You do not need to be delivered from evil. Can't you see? It's me. Me—I who am so close to being swallowed up in all that eternal darkness. But I didn't say it. I wasn't angry at her—just deadly tired.

In the light of the next day, I tried to tell myself that I had only imagined the great evil of the scene the night before. Hadn't I once tried to convince Call that the Captain was a Nazi—a U-boat delivered spy? Why, then, was I so upset over Grandma's accusation? I saw again in my mind those glittering eyes and knew it was not the same. Grandma, however, seemed to have forgotten everything. She was quite her grumpy, silly self again, and we were relieved to pretend that we, too, had forgotten.

In February, Call dropped out of school. His mother and grandmother were destitute, and my father offered to take him aboard the *Portia Sue* as an oyster culler. My father would tong, bringing up oysters with his long firwood tongs, which looked like scissors with a metal rake at the end of each shaft. He would open the rakes and drop his catch onto the wooden culling board. There

Call, his hands in heavy rubber gloves, would cull, using a culling hammer. With the hammer head he knocked off the excess shell, and with the blade at the other end he struck off the small oysters. The debris was shoved into the Bay and the good oysters forward until they could be sold to a buy boat, which would take them to market. From Monday well before dawn to Saturday night, they would be gone, sleeping all week on cramped bunks in the *Portia Sue's* tiny cabin, for the best oyster beds were up the Eastern Shore rivers, too far away for daily commuting when gas was so strictly rationed.

Of course I was jealous of Call, but I was surprised to realize how very much I missed him. All my life my father had followed the water, so it had never seemed strange to have him gone, but Call had always been around, either with me or close by. Now we only saw him at church.

Caroline made a fuss over him every Sunday. "My, Call, we sure do miss you." How could she know? Besides, it didn't seem quite ladylike to say something like that, straight out.

Each week, he seemed to grow taller and thinner, and his hands were turning more and more into the rough brown bark of a waterman's. Even his manner seemed to change. The solemnity that had always lent him, as a small child, a rather comic air, now seemed a sort of youthful dignity. You could sense his pride that he had come at last into a man's estate, the sole support of the women upon whom he had until now depended. I knew we had been growing apart since summer, but I had been able to blame that on Caroline. Now it was more painful, for the very things that made him stronger and more attractive were taking him deep into the world of men— a place I could never hope to enter.

Later that winter I began going again to see the Captain. I always went with Caroline. It wouldn't have been proper for either of us to go alone. He taught us how to play poker, which I had to be persuaded to do, but once I began it made me feel deliciously wicked. He probably owned the only deck of regular playing cards on Rass. Those were the days when good Methodists only indulged in Rook or Old Maid. We played poker for toothpicks, as though they were gold pieces. At least I did. Nothing gave me greater satisfaction than totally cleaning out my sister. It must have shown, because I can remember her saying on more than one occasion in a very annoyed tone of voice, "For goodness' sakes, Wheeze, it's only a game" as I would lick my chops and scrape all her tumbled stacks of toothpicks across the table with my arm.

One day after a particularly satisfying win, the Captain turned from me to Caroline and said, "I miss your singing now that Trudy's gone. Those were some happy times."

Caroline smiled. "I liked them too," she said.

"You're not letting down on your practicing now, are you?"

"Oh," she said. "I don't know. I guess it's all right."

"You're doing fine." I was impatient to get on to another game.

She shook her head. "I really miss my lessons," she said. "I hadn't realized how much they meant."

"Well, it's a pity," I said the way a grown-up speaks to a child to shut her up. "Times are hard."

"Yes," the Captain said. "I suppose lessons take a lot of money."

"It's not just the money," I said quickly, trying to ignore the vision of my own little hoard of bills and change. "It's the gas and all. Once you get to Crisfield, it's worth your life to get a taxi. Now if the county would just send us to boarding school like they do the Smith Island kids—"

"Oh, Wheeze, that wouldn't help. What kind of a music program could they have at that school? We beat them all to pieces in the contest last year."

"Well, we should be able to request a special school on account of special circumstances."

"They'd never pay for us to go to any school, much less a really good school," she said sadly.

"Well, they ought to." I wanted to dump the blame on the county and deal the cards. "Don't you think they should, Captain?"

"Yes, somebody should."

"But they won't," I said. "Anything dumber than a blowfish, it's a county board of education."

They laughed, and to my relief the subject was closed. It was too bad about Caroline's lessons, but she'd had a couple of good years at Salisbury. Besides, it wasn't my' fault. I hadn't started the war or caused the storm.

The Captain did not come to our house. He was invited perfunctorily every Sunday, but he seemed to know that he oughtn't to come and always managed an excuse. So I was startled one afternoon a week or so later to see him hurrying up the path to our porch, his face flushed with what looked like excitement and not just the effects of his rushing. I opened the door before he had stepped up onto the porch.

"Sara Louise," he said, waving a letter in his hand as he came. "Such wonderful news!" He paused at the door. "Your father's not here, I guess." I shook my head. It was only Wednesday. "Well, please get your mother. I can't wait." He was beaming all over.

Grandma was rocking in her chair, reading or pretending to read her large leather-bound Bible. He nodded at her. "Miss Louise," he said. She didn't look up. Mother and Caroline were coming in from the kitchen.

"Why, Captain Wallace," said my mother, wiping her hands on her apron. "Sit down. Louise, Caroline, will you fix some tea for the Captain?"

"No, no," he said. "Sit down, all of you. I've got the most wonderful news. I can't wait."

We all sat down.

He put the letter on his lap and pressed out a crease with his fingertip. "There are so few opportunities for young people on this island," he began. "I'm sure, Miss Susan, a woman of your background and education must suffer to see her children deprived."

154

What was he leading up to? I could feel a faint stir of excitement in my breast.

"You know how much I think of you, how indebted both Trudy and I are—were—to all of you. And now—" He could hardly contain himself. He smiled at me. "I have Sara Louise to thank for the idea. You see, Trudy left a little legacy. I didn't know what to do with it, because I swore to myself I would never touch her money. There isn't a great deal, but there is enough for a good boarding school." He was beaming all over. "I've investigated. There will be enough for Caroline to go to Baltimore and continue her music. Nothing would make Trudy happier than that, I know."

I sat there as stunned as though he had thrown a rock in my face. Caroline!

Caroline jumped up and ran over and threw her arms around his neck.

"Caroline, wait," my mother was saying. Surely she would point out that she had two daughters. "Captain, this is very generous, but I can't—I'd have to talk with my husband. I couldn't—"

"We must convince him, Miss Susan. Sara Louise, tell her how you were saying to me just the other day that someone should understand that special circumstances demand special solutions—that Caroline ought to be sent to a really good school where she could continue her music. Isn't that right, Sara Louise?"

I made a funny sound in my throat that must have

resembled a "yes." The Captain took it for approval. My grandmother twisted in her chair to look at me. I looked away as fast as I could. She was smiling.

"Isn't that right, Sara Louise?" she asked in a voice intended to mimic the Captain's. "Isn't that right?"

I jumped toward the kitchen with the excuse of making tea. I could hear the Captain talking on to Mother and Caroline about the academy he knew in Baltimore with the wonderful music program. The words roared in my ears like a storm wind. I put the kettle on and laid out cups and spoons. Everything seemed so heavy I could hardly pick them up. I struggled to pry the lid from the can of tea leaves, aware that my grandmother had come in and was standing close behind me. I stiffened at the sound of her hoarse whisper.

"Romans nine thirteen," she said. " 'As it is written, Jacob have I loved, but Esau have I hated.' "

15

I served the tea with a smile sunk in concrete pilings.

"Thank you, Louise," my mother said.

The Captain nodded at me as he took his cup off the tray. Caroline, distracted with happiness, seemed not to see me at all. I took the cup that I had prepared for her back to the kitchen, brushing past my grandmother, who was grinning at me in the doorway. After I had put down the tray, I had to squeeze past her once more to get to the protection of my room. "Jacob have I loved—" she began, but I hurried by and up the steps as quickly as I could.

I closed the door behind me. Then, without thinking, I took off my dress and hung it up and put on my nightgown. I crawled under the covers and closed my eyes. It was half-past three in the afternoon.

I suppose I meant never to get up again, but of course I did. At suppertime my mother came in to ask if I were ill, and being too slow-witted to invent an ailment, I got up and went down to the meal. No one said much at the table. Caroline was positively glowing, my mother quiet and thoughtful, my grandmother grinning and stealing little peeks at my face.

At bedtime Caroline finally remembered that she had a sister. "Please don't mind too much, Wheeze. It means so much to me."

I just shook my head, not trusting myself to reply. Why should it matter if I minded? How would that change anything? The Captain, who I'd always believed was different, had, like everyone else, chosen her over me. Since the day we were born, twins like Jacob and Esau, the younger had ruled the older. Did anyone ever say Esau and Jacob?

"Jacob have I loved . . ." Suddenly my stomach flipped. Who was speaking? I couldn't remember the passage. Was it Isaac, the father of the twins? No, even the Bible said that Isaac had favored Esau. Rebecca, the mother, perhaps. It was her conniving that helped Jacob steal the blessing from his brother. Rebecca—I had hated her from childhood, but somehow I knew that these were not her words.

I got up, pulled the black out curtains, and turned on the table lamp between our beds.

"Wheeze?" Caroline propped herself up on one elbow and blinked at me.

"Just have to see something." I took my Bible from our little crate bookcase, and bringing it over to the light, looked up the passage Grandma had cited. Romans, the ninth chapter and the thirteenth verse. The speaker was God.

I was shaking all over as I closed the book and got back under the covers. There was, then, no use struggling or even trying. It was God himself who hated me. And without cause. "Therefore," verse eighteen had gone on to rub it in, "hath he mercy on whom he will have mercy, and whom he will he hardeneth." God had chosen to hate me. And if my heart was hard, that was his doing as well.

My mother did not hate me. The next two days part of me watched her watching me. She wanted to speak to me, I could tell, but my heart was already beginning to harden and I avoided her.

Then Friday after supper while Caroline was practicing, she followed me up to the room.

"I need to talk with you, Louise."

I grunted rudely. She flinched but didn't correct me. "I've been giving this business a lot of thought," she said.

"What business?" I was determined to be cruel.

"The offer—the idea of Caroline going to school in Baltimore."

I watched her coldly, my right hand at my mouth.

"It—it—well, it is a wonderful chance for her, you know. A chance we, your father and I, could never hope— Louise?"

"Yes?" I bit down savagely on a hang nail and ripped it so deeply that the blood started.

"Don't do that to your finger, please."

I grabbed my hand from my mouth. What did she

want from me? My permission? My blessing?

"I-I was trying to think—we could never afford this school in Baltimore, but maybe Crisfield. We could borrow something on next year's earnings—"

"Why should Caroline go to Crisfield when she has a chance—"

"No, not Caroline, you. I thought we might send you—"

She did hate me. There. See. She was trying to get rid of me. "Crisfield!" I cried contemptuously. "Crisfield! I'd rather be chopped for crab bait!"

"Oh," she said. I had plainly confused her. "I really thought you might like—"

"Well, you were wrong!"

"Louise—"

"Momma, would you just get out and leave me alone!" If she refused, I would take it for a sign, not only that she cared about me but that God did. If she stayed in that room— She stood up, hesitating.

"Why don't you just go?"

"All right, Louise, if that's what you want." She closed the door quietly behind her.

My father came home as usual on Saturday. He and my mother spent most of Sunday afternoon at the Captain's. I don't know how the matter was settled in a way that satisfied my father's proud independence, but by the time they returned it was settled. Within two weeks we were on the dock to see Caroline off to Baltimore. She kissed us all, including the Captain and Call, who turned the color of steamed crab at her touch. She was back for summer vacation a few days before Call left for the navy, at which time she provided the island with another great show of kissing and carrying on. You couldn't doubt that she'd go far in grand opera judging by that performance.

After Call left, I gave up progging and took over the responsibility of my father's crab floats. I poled my skiff from float to float, fishing out the soft crabs and taking them to the crab house to pack them in boxes filled with eelgrass for shipping. I knew almost as much about blue crabs as a seasoned waterman. One look at a crab's swimming leg and I could tell almost to the hour when the critter was going to shed. The next to the last section is nearly transparent and if the crab is due to moult in less than a couple of weeks, the faint line of the new shell can be seen growing there beneath the present one. It's called a "white sign." Gradually, the shadow darkens. When a waterman catches a "pink sign," he knows the moulting will take place in about a week, so he gently breaks the crab's big claws to keep it from killing all its neighbors and brings it home to finish peeling in his floats. A "red sign" will begin to shed in a matter of hours and a "buster" has already begun.

Shedding its shell is a long and painful business for a big Jimmy, but for a she-crab, turning into a sook, it seemed somehow worse. I'd watch them there in the float, knowing once they shed that last time and turned into grown-up lady crabs there was nothing left for them. They hadn't even had a Jimmy make love to them. Poor sooks. They'd never take a trip down the Bay to lay their eggs before they died. The fact that there wasn't much future for the Jimmies once they were packed in eelgrass didn't bother me so much. Males, I thought, always have a chance to live no matter how short their lives, but females, ordinary, ungifted ones, just get soft and die.

At about seven I would head home for breakfast and then back to the crab house and floats until our four-thirty supper. After supper sometimes one of my parents would go back with me, but more often I went alone. I didn't really mind. It made me feel less helpless to be a girl of fifteen doing what many regarded as a man's job. When school started in the fall, I, like every boy on Rass over twelve, was simply too busy to think of enrolling. My parents objected, but I assured them that when the crab season was over, I would go and catch up with the class. Secretly, I wasn't sure that I could stand school with neither Caroline nor Call there with me, but, of course, I didn't mention this to my parents.

We had another severe storm that September. It took no lives, in the literal sense, but since it took another six to eight feet of fast land off the southern end of the island, four families whose houses were in jeopardy moved to the mainland. They were followed within the month by two other families who had never quite recovered from the storm of '42. There was plenty of war work on the mainland for both men and women at what seemed to us to be unbelievable wages. So as the water nibbled away at our land, the war nibbled away at our souls. We were lucky, though. In the Bay we could still work without fear. Fishermen off the Atlantic coast were being stalked by submarines. Some were killed, though we like the rest of the country were kept ignorant of those bodies that washed ashore just a few miles to the east of us.

Our first war deaths did not come until the fall of 1943, but then there were three at once when three island boys who had signed aboard the same ship were lost off a tiny island in the South Pacific that none of us had ever heard of before.

I did not pray anymore. I had even stopped going to church. At first I thought my parents would put up a fight when one Sunday morning I just didn't come back from the crab house in time for church. My grandmother lit into me at suppertime, but to my surprise my father quietly took my part. I was old enough, he said, to decide for myself. When she launched into prophecies of eternal damnation, he told her that God was my judge, not they. He meant it as a kindness, for how could he know that God had judged me before I was born and had cast me out before I took my first breath? I did not miss church, but sometimes I wished I might pray. I wanted, oddly enough, to pray for Call. I was so afraid he might die in some alien ocean thousands of miles from home.

If I was being prayed for mightily at Wednesday night prayer meetings, I was not told of it. I suppose people were a little afraid of me. I must have been a strange sight, always dressed in man's work clothes, my hands as rough and weathered as the sides of the crab house where I worked.

It was the last week in November when the first northwest blow of winter sent the egg-laden sooks rushing toward Virginia and the Jimmies deep under the Chesapeake mud. My father took a few days off to shoot duck, and then put the culling board back on the *Portia Sue* and headed out for oysters. One week in school that fall had been enough for me and one week alone on the oyster beds was enough for him. We hardly discussed it. I just got up at two Monday morning, dressed as warmly as I could with a change of clothes in a gunnysack. We ate breakfast together, my mother serving us. No one said anything about my not being a man—maybe they'd forgotten.

I suppose if I were to try to stick a pin through that most elusive spot "the happiest days of my life," that strange winter on the *Portia Sue* with my father would have to be indicated. I was not happy in any way that would make sense to most people, but I was, for the first time in my life, deeply content with what life was giving me. Part of it was the discoveries—who would have believed that my father sang while tonging? My quiet, unassuming father, whose voice could hardly be heard in church, stood there in his oilskins, his rubber-gloved hands on his tongs, and sang to the oysters. It was a wonderful sound, deep and pure. He knew the

Methodist hymnbook by heart. "The crabs now, they don't crave music, but oysters," he explained shyly, "there's nothing they favor more than a purty tune." And he would serenade the oysters of Chesapeake Bay with the hymns the brothers Wesley had written to bring sinners to repentance and praise. Part of my deep contentment was due, I'm sure, to being with my father, but part, too, was that I was no longer fighting. My sister was gone, my grandmother a fleeting Sunday apparition, and God, if not dead, far removed from my concern.

It was work that did this for me. I had never had work before that sucked from me every breath, every thought, every trace of energy.

"I wish," said my father one night as we were eating our meager supper in the cabin, "I wish you could do a little studying of a night. You know, keep up your schooling."

We both glanced automatically at the kerosene lamp, which was more smell than light. "I'd be too tired," I said.

"I reckon."

It had been one of our longer conversations. Yet once again I was a member of a good team. We were averaging ten bushels of oysters a day. If it kept up, we'd have a record year. We did not compare ourselves to the skipjacks, the large sailboats with five or six crew members, that raked dredges across the bottom to harvest a heavy load of muck and trash and bottom spat along with oysters each time the mechanical winch cranked up a dredge.

We tongers stood perched on the washboards of our tiny boats, and, just as our fathers and grandfathers had before us, used our fir wood tongs, three or four times taller than our own bodies, to reach down gently to the oyster bed, feel the bottom until we came to a patch of market-sized oysters, and then closing the rakes over the catch, bringing it up to the culling board. Of course, we could not help but bring up some spat, as every oyster clings to its bed until the culling hammer forces a separation, but compared to the dredge, we left the precious bottom virtually undisturbed to provide a bed for the oysters that would be harvested by our children's children.

At first, I was only a culler, but if we found a rich bed, I'd tong as well, and then when the culling board was loaded, I'd bring in my last tong full hand over hand, dump it on the board, and cull until I'd caught up with my father.

Oysters are not the mysterious creatures that blue crabs are. You can learn about them more quickly. In a few hours, I could measure a three-inch shell with my eyes. Below three inches they have to go back. A live oyster, a good one, when it hits the culling board has a tightly closed shell. You throw away the open ones. They're dead already. I was a good oyster in those days. Not even the presence at Christmastime of a radiant, grown-up Caroline could get under my shell.

The water began to freeze in late February. I could see my culling like a trail behind us on the quickly forming ice patches. "Them slabs will grow together blessed quick," my father said. And without further discussion, he turned the boat. We stopped only long enough to sell our scanty harvest to a buy boat along the way and then headed straight for Rass. The temperature was dropping fast. By morning we were frozen in tight.

There followed two weeks of impossible weather. My father made no attempt to take the *Portia Sue* out. The first day or so I was content simply to sleep away some of the accumulated exhaustion of the winter. But the day soon came when my mother, handing me a ten o'clock cup of coffee, was suggesting mildly that I might want to take in a few days of school since the bad weather was likely to hold out for some time.

Her kindly intended words lay on me like a wet sail. I tried to appear calm, but I was caught and suffocated by the idea of returning to school. Didn't she realize that I was by now a hundred years older than anyone there, including Miss Hazel? I put my coffee down, sloshing it over the saucer onto the table. Coffee was rationed then and to waste it, inexcusable. I jumped up mumbling an apology to get a rag, but she was quicker and began sponging the brown liquid off the oilcloth before I could move, so I sat down again and let her do it.

"I worry about you, Louise," she said, mopping carefully and not looking at me. "Your father and I are grateful, indeed. I hardly know what we'd have done without you. But—" She trailed off, reluctant, I suppose, to predict what might become of me if I went on in my present manner of life. I didn't know whether to seem touched or annoyed. I was certainly irritated. If they were willing to accept the fruits of my life, they should at least spare me the burden of their guilt.

"I don't want to go back to school," I said evenly.

"But—"

"You can teach me here. You're a teacher."

"But you're so lonely."

"I'd be lonelier there. I've never belonged at that school." I was becoming, much to my own displeasure, a bit heated as I spoke. "I hate them and they hate me." There. I had overstated my case. They had never cared enough about me one way or the other to hate me. I might have from time to time served as the butt of their laughter, but I had never achieved enough status to earn their hatred.

She straightened up, sighing, and went over to the sink to wash the coffee from her cloth. "I suppose I could," she said finally. "Teach you, I mean, if Miss Hazel would lend me the books. Captain Wallace might be willing to do the math."

"Can't you do that?" Although I was no longer in love with the Captain, I did not wish to be thrown in such close company with him again—just the two of us. There was a residue of pain there.

"No," she said. "If you want to be taught at home, I'd have to ask someone else to do the math. There is no one else with the—with the time." She was always very careful not to seem to sneer at the rest of the islanders for their lack of education.

I'm not sure how my mother persuaded Miss Hazel to go along with the arrangement. The woman was very jealous of her position as the one high school teacher on Rass. Perhaps my mother argued that my irregular attendance would be disruptive, I don't know, but she came home with the books, and we began our kitchen-table school.

As for my lessons with the Captain, my mother, sensitive to the least hint of inappropriate behavior, always went with me. She would sit and knit while we had our very proper lesson, no more poker or jokes, and afterward, she and the Captain would chat across my head. He was always eager for news of Caroline, who was prospering in Baltimore as the Prophet Jeremiah claimed only the wicked do. Her letters were few and hurried but filled with details of her conquests. In turn, the Captain would share news from Call, from whom he heard nearly as often as we heard from Caroline. Between letters there was a lot of "Did I remember to tell you . . .?" or "Did I read the part about . . .?" Censorship kept Call from revealing very much about where he was or what was going on, but in what he didn't say there was enough to make my flesh crawl. The Captain, having been through naval battles before, seemed to regard the whole thing with more interest than fear.

There were only a few more days of oystering left that winter of '44. During the end of March and most of April, my father caught and salted alewives for crab bait, overhauled the motor on the *Portia Sue,* and converted it once more for crabbing. After he had caught and salted his crab bait, he did a little fishing to pass the days and even some house repairs. I crammed in as much schooling at home as possible, because once the crabs were moving, I'd be back on duty at the floats and in the crab house.

My mother heard the report of D day on our ancient radio and walked up to the crab house to tell me. She seemed more excited than I, to whom it signified only more war and killing. Besides, it was not the European war that concerned me.

16

Roosevelt was elected to a fourth term in the fall of 1944 without the help of Rass, which went solidly Republican as usual. And yet, when he died the following April, we shared the shock of the nation. As I heard the news, I remembered instantly the day the war had begun, Caroline and I standing hand in hand before the radio. The chill that went through me was the same coldness of that winter day in 1941 when Caroline and I had begun to grow up.

Some days after Roosevelt's death, I received the only letter I had ever gotten from Call. I was surprised to see how my hands trembled opening it, so much that I was obliged to turn my back on my mother and grandmother in the living room and go to the kitchen. It was very brief.

> Dear Wheeze,
>   What do you think St. Peter said to Franklin D. Roosevelt? Get it?
>
>   Call

I got it, but as was usually the case with Call's jokes, I didn't find it the least bit funny.

On April 30, the day that Hitler committed suicide, I was permitted to take the exams for graduation. I passed, much to my satisfaction, with the highest grades recorded from Rass. Not that Miss Hazel told my mother this. It was the mainland school supervisor who had graded the exams who took time to write me a note of congratulations.

When the war in Europe ended eight days later, it was overshadowed by the news from Baltimore that Caroline had been accepted by the Juilliard School of Music in New York on a full scholarship.

I looked upon this announcement with enormous relief as the end of any sacrifice I would ever be asked to make for Caroline. My parents hoped it meant that she could take a rest and come home for the summer, but she wrote at the last minute to say that she had been offered a chance to go to summer school at Peabody—an opportunity her voice teacher felt she must not pass up. I'm sure my parents were disappointed, but I was not. The war was coming quickly to a close. Soon, I felt sure, Call would be back.

Exactly what Call's return would mean to me, I could not say. I had not despised my life of the past two years, but I began to realize that it had been a time of hibernation, for I felt stirrings I had almost forgotten. Perhaps when Call came home—perhaps—well, at the very least when he came I could turn over my tasks to him. My father would be overjoyed to have a man to help him. And I—what was it I wanted? I could leave the island, if I wished. I could see the mountains. I could even take a job in Washington or Baltimore if I wanted to. If I chose to leave—there was something cold about the idea, but I shook it away.

I began to cream my hands each night, sloshing lotion all over them and sleeping in a pair of mother's worn white cotton gloves—perhaps the pair she was married in. Is that possible? It was stupid, I decided, to resign myself to being another Auntie Braxton. I was young and able, as my exams had proved. Without God, or a man, I could still conquer a small corner of the world— if I wanted to. My hands stubbornly refused to be softened. But I was determined not to give up on them this time.

Something was happening inside of Grandma, too. Suddenly that summer she decided that my mother was the woman who had stolen her husband. One afternoon I came in for supper from the crab house to find Momma trying to bake bread. I say trying, because it was a sweltering August day, which was hard enough to fight on the island, but as Momma worked, her face shining with sweat, her hair plastered against her head, Grandma was reading aloud to her, in a voice that could be heard from the street, the section in Proverbs chapter six entitled, "The mischiefs of whoredom."

" 'Can a man take fire in his bosom, and his clothes not be burned?' " my grandmother was crying out as I came into the back door. We were used to Grandma reading the Bible to us, but the selections were not usually quite so purple. I didn't even understand what it was all about until Grandma, seeing that I had come in, said, "Tell that viperish adulteress to listen to God's Word!" And proceeded to read on into chapter seven, which details the seduction of a young man by a "strange woman."

I looked down at my poor mother, struggling to pull several loaves of bread out of the oven. It was all I could do to keep from bursting out laughing. Susan Bradshaw as a scarlet woman? It's a joke, get it? I began banging pots and pans, more to cover my giggles than to help with supper.

I looked up to see my father in the front doorway. He seemed to be waiting there, taking in the scene, before he determined what his part should be.

Grandma had not seen him. She stumbled on through the passage. " 'He goeth after her straightway, as an ox to the slaughter . . .' "

Without even removing his boots, my father walked straight across the living room to the kitchen and, pretending not to care who watched, kissed my mother on her neck where a tendril of hair had pulled loose from her bun. I blushed despite myself, but he didn't seem to notice me. He whispered something into her ear. She gave a wry grin.

" 'Till a dart strike through his liver . . .' "

"Liver?" My father mouthed the word in mock horror. Then he turned to Grandma, all teasing dropped.

"Mother. I think your supper is on the table."

She seemed a little startled by his voice, but she came to the table determined to finish the terrible passage, yet not willing to miss her supper to do so. " 'Her house is the way to hell—' " My father took the Bible gently from her hands and put it on a bookshelf above her head.

She twisted away from him like a startled child, but he took her arm and led her to the table and held her chair for her. The gesture seemed to satisfy her. She directed a triumphant look at my mother and then set herself with great energy to her food.

My father smiled across the table at my mother. She pushed her wet hair off her face and smiled back. I turned away from the sight. Don't look at each other like that. Grandma might see you. But was it only the fear of Grandma's foolish jealousies that made me want to weep?

It was, ironically, the news of Hiroshima that made our lives easier. My grandmother, catching somehow the ultimate terror that the bomb promised, turned from adultery to Armageddon. We were all admonished to fight the whore of Babylon, who was somehow identified in Grandma's mind with the pope of the Roman Catholic Church, and repeatedly warned to prepare to meet our God. A rapid scurrying through her well-worn Bible and she had located several passages to shake over our heads— telling us of the sun turning to darkness and the moon to blood. How could she know that the Day of the Lord's Anger was an almost welcome relief from her accusations of lust and adultery? There never had been any Catholics on Rass, and the end of all things was, after all, almost unimaginable, and therefore had far less power to shake one's core.

We did not take a holiday when peace was declared. There were still crabs moving in the Bay and peeling in the floats. But we ate our supper with a special delight. Toward the end of the meal, my father, turning to me as though peace had brought with it some great change to our meager fortunes, said, "Well, Louise, what will you do now?"

"Do?" Was he trying to get rid of me?

"Yes," he said. "You're a young woman now. I can't keep you on as a hand much longer."

"I don't mind," I said. "I like the water."

"I mind," he said quietly. "But I'm grateful to have had you with me."

"When Call comes back," my mother said as my heart fluttered at the words, "when Call comes back he could lend a hand and you could take a trip. Wouldn't you like that?"

A trip. I'd never been farther than Salisbury.

"You might go to New York and see Caroline." She was getting excited for me.

"Maybe," I said. I wouldn't hurt her by saying that I had no desire to see either New York or my sister. There was that old dream of mountains. Maybe I would go far enough to see a mountain.

At the tail end of the crab season Call came home. I was still at the crab house, but bored with lack of crabs to watch and pack, when suddenly the light from the doorway was blocked. The body of a large man in uniform was filling the door. There was a bass laugh that sounded vaguely familiar and a voice. "Crabby as ever, I see," it said. And then, "Get it?"

"Call!" I jumped, nearly tripping over a stack of packing boxes. He was holding out both his arms, inviting an embrace, but I was suddenly shy. "Oh, my blessed, Call. You done growed up," I said to cover my confusion.

"That's what the navy promised," he said.

I was aware of his clean, masculine smell and at the same time of the smell of salt water and crab, which was my only perfume. I wiped my hands on my pants. "Let's get out of here," I said.

He glanced around. "Can you leave?"

"Mercy, yes," I said. "I don't get more'n a boxful every couple hours."

We walked the board planking to where the skiff was tied. He handed me down into the bow as if I were a lady. Then he jumped into the stern and took up the pole. He stood there in his petty officer's uniform, tall and almost shockingly broad-shouldered and thin-hipped, his cap pushed slightly back, the sun lighting on the patch of reddish hair that showed. His eyes were bright blue and smiling down at me, and his nose had mysteriously shrunk to fit his face. I realized that I was staring at him and that he was enjoying it. I looked away, embarrassed.

He laughed. "You haven't changed, you know." If he'd

meant it as a compliment he couldn't have failed more. He himself had changed so marvelously over the past two years, surely something should have happened to me. I crossed my arms over my chest and held my hands tightly under the protection of my upper arms. They scratched like dry sand.

"Aren't you going to ask me about myself?" I had the feeling he was trying to tease me about something. I didn't like it.

"Well," I said, trying not to sound irritated. "Tell me where you been and what you saw."

"I think I seen every island in the world," he said.

"And you come home to the purtiest one of all," I answered.

"Yeah," he said, but his focus blurred for a moment. "The water's about to get her, Wheeze."

"Only a bit, to the south," I said defensively.

"Wheeze, open your eyes," he said. "In two years I've been gone, she's lost at least an acre. Another good storm—"

It wasn't right. He should have been more loyal. You don't come home after two years away and suddenly inform your mother that she's dying. I don't know what he saw in my face, but what I actually said was, "I guess you been to see the Captain already."

"No. That's why I came to get you. So we could go see him together like we used to." He shifted the pole to port side. "I guess he's gotten a lot older, huh?"

"What would you expect?"

"Crabby as ever, huh?" He repeated, trying to make it sound like a joke, to tease me out of my mood.

"He's nearly eighty," I said, and added, "I leave the skiff at the slip now. It's handier than the gut."

He nodded and steered toward the main dock.

"Miss Trudy's death took a lot out of him, didn't it?"

He was beginning to annoy me as much as he had when he was a chubby boy. "I wouldn't say that."

He squinted down at me. "Well, it did, you know. Caroline and I both remarked on it. He was never the same after that."

"Caroline," I said, so anxious to change the subject I was even willing to speak of my sister's good fortune, "Caroline is at a music school in New York City."

"Juilliard," he said. "Yes, I know."

We were at the slip now. I wanted to ask how he knew, but I was afraid to. So I jumped out and tied up the skiff, next to where my father would tie the *Portia Sue*. He shipped the pole and climbed out after me.

We walked without talking down the narrow street. When we got to our gate, I stopped. "I'd like to change my clothes before I go calling."

"Sure," he said.

I carried a pitcher of water to the washstand upstairs to bathe as best I could from the basin. Below I could hear Call's new deep voice rumbling in reply to my mother's soft alto. Every now and then a staccato interjection from my grandmother. I strained to make out the words but couldn't through the door. When I put on my Sunday dress, which I hadn't worn for almost two years, it strained across my breasts and shoulders. I could hardly bring myself to look in the mirror, first at my brown face and then at my sun-scorched hair. I dampened it with water and tried to coax it into a few waves about my forehead. I slopped hand lotion all over my hands and then on my face and legs, even my arms and elbows. It had a cheap fragrance, which I tried to fool myself would cover the essence of crab.

I nearly stumbled on the stairs. All three of them looked up. My mother smiled and would have spoken—her mouth was pursed with some encouraging comment— but I glared her into silence.

Call stood up. "Now," he said. "That is an improvement." It was not the encouragement needed at that moment.

My grandmother half rose from the rocker, "Where you going with that man, Louise? Huh? Where you going?" I grabbed Call's elbow and shoved him toward the door.

He was laughing silently as the voice followed us out onto the porch. He shook his head at me, as though we were sharing a joke. "I see she hasn't changed, either," he said at the gate.

"She's worse. The things she calls Momma . . ."

"Well," he said, "you mustn't take it to heart," dismissing the years of aggravation with a flick of his hand.

The Captain greeted me with courtesy, but he was overjoyed to see Call. He embraced him almost as though Call were a woman. Men on Rass did not hug each other, but Call returned the embrace without any sign of embarrassment. I could see tears glittering in the old man's eyes when at last he pulled away.

"Well," he said. "My. Well."

"It's good to be back," Call said, covering the old man's discomposure.

"I've saved a tin of milk," the Captain said. "Saved against this day." He started for the kitchen. "Let me just put on the kettle."

"Do you want some help?" I asked, half-rising.

"Oh, no, no. You sit right there and entertain our conquering hero." Call laughed. "You heard about Caroline?" the Captain called.

"Yessir, and she's everlastingly grateful to you."

"It was Trudy's money. Nothing would have made Trudy happier than to know she helped Caroline go on with her music." There was a pause. Then he stuck his head in the doorway. "You been keeping up with each other lately?"

"I saw her," Call said. "I stopped in New York on the way home."

My body understood long before my mind did. First it chilled, then it began to burn, with my heart thumping overtime in alarm.

They were exchanging inanities about the size and terrors of New York, but my body knew that the conversa-

181

tion was about something far more threatening. The Captain brought in the black tea and the tin of milk, which he had neatly poked open with an ice pick—two holes on one side, one on the other.

"I'm guessing you can take the tea now," he said, handing a chipped cup and saucer, first to me, and then to Call. "Not just the milk."

"That's right," Call said grinning. "They made me a man."

"So." The Captain seated himself carefully, and compensating for the tremor in his hands, slowly lifted his own cup to his mouth and took a long sip. "So. What's Miss Caroline got to say for herself these days?"

Call's face flamed in pleasure. It was the question he had been bursting to answer. "She—she said, 'Yes.' "

I knew, of course, what he meant. There was no need to press him to explain. But something compelled me to hear my own doom spelled out. " 'Yes' to what?" I asked.

"Let's just say," he was eyeing the Captain slyly. "Let's just say she answered her Call."

The Captain gave a great tuba laugh, sloshing his tea out onto his lap. He patted away at it with his free hand, still laughing.

"Get it?" Call turned to me. "She answered—"

"I guess it took you most of the train trip from New York to work that one out." Call stopped smiling. I suppose it was the bitterness in my tone. "She's only seventeen," I said, trying to justify myself.

"Eighteen in January." As though I needed to be told. "My mother was married at fifteen."

"So was my grandmother," I said nastily. "Great advertisement for early marriage, wouldn't you say?"

"Sara Louise." The Captain was almost whispering. I stood up so quickly that the room seemed to spin. I grabbed the arm of the chair, rattling the tea cup all around the saucer. I staggered to the kitchen and put it down, then came back into the room. I knew I was making a scene, but I didn't know how to escape it. How unjust to throw everything at me at once.

"Well," I said, "I guess you won't be culling for Daddy this winter."

"No," he said. "I've got a part-time job lined up in New York as soon as I'm discharged. With that and my GI Bill, I can go to school there."

"What about Caroline's school? Have you thought of her? What she'll have to give up to marry you?"

"Oh, my blessed," he said. "It's not like that. I'd never let her give up her chance to sing. She'll go ahead with all her plans. I wouldn't ever hold her back. Surely you know that, Wheeze." He was asking me humbly to understand. "I can help her. I can—"

"Give her a safe harbor," the Captain offered quietly.

"Caroline?" I snorted.

"She's alone in that world, Wheeze. She needs me."

You? I was thinking. You, Call? I said nothing, but he heard me anyhow.

"I guess," he was saying softly, "I guess it's hard for

you to think someone like Caroline might favor me." He gave a short laugh. "You never did think I was much to brag about, now did you?"

Oh, God. If I had believed in God I could have cursed him and died. As it was, I extricated myself as quickly as I could from them and made my way, not home, but back to the crab house where I proceeded to ruin my only decent dress fishing the floats.

17

Call was not discharged as soon as he had hoped, so it was the next year, the day before Christmas 1946, that he and Caroline were married. My parents went up for the ceremony in the Juilliard chapel, which, I gathered, was stark in word and dress, but rich in Bach and Mozart, thanks to Caroline's school friends.

I stayed home with Grandma. It was my choice. My parents spoke of getting a neighbor to stay with her, and each offered to remain and let me go instead. But I felt they were greatly relieved by my insistence. The way Grandma was or could be, we dreaded the thought of asking someone outside the family to endure even a few days alone with her. Besides, as they said later, it was the first trip of any length that the two of them had ever taken together. They left, with apologies to me, on the twenty-second. Perhaps my soul, now as calloused as my hands, could have borne such a wedding. I don't know. I was glad not to be put to the test.

Grandma was like a child whose parents have gone off and left her without making plain where they have gone or when they could be expected to return. "Where's Truitt?"

"He's gone to New York for Caroline's wedding, Grandma."

She looked blank, as though she were not quite sure who Caroline was but felt she shouldn't ask. She rocked quietly for a few minutes, picking a thread on her knitted shawl. "Where's Susan?"

"She went with Daddy to New York."

"New York?"

"For Caroline's wedding."

"I know," she snapped. "Why did they leave me?"

"Because you hate to ride the ferry, Grandma, especially in the wintertime."

"I hate the water." She dully observed the worn-out ritual. Suddenly she stopped rocking and cocked her head at me. "Why are you here?"

"You hate to be alone, Grandma."

"Humph." She sniffed and pulled the shawl tight about her shoulders. "I don't need to be watched like one of your old peelers."

The image of Grandma as an old sook caught in my mind. *Get it?* I wanted to say to somebody.

"What you cutting on?"

"Oh, just whittling." It was in fact a branch of almost straight driftwood, which I had decided would make a good cane for Grandma. I had spread out part of the Sunday *Sun* and was trimming the wood down before sanding it.

"I ain't seen that old heathen about," she said. "I guess he's dead like everybody else."

"No. Captain Wallace is just fine."

"He don't ever come around here." She sighed. "Too snobby to pay attention to the likes of me, I reckon."

I stopped whittling. "I thought you didn't like him, Grandma."

"No, I don't favor him. He thinks he's the cat's pajamas. Too good for the daughter of a man who don't even own his own boat."

"What are you talking about, Grandma?"

"He never paid me no mind. Old heathen."

I felt as though I had stumbled off a narrow path right into a marsh. "Grandma, do you mean *now?*"

"You was always a ignorant child. I wouldn't have him on a silver plate *now*. I mean *then*."

"Grandma," I was still trying to feel my way, "you were a lot younger than the Captain."

She flashed her eyes at me. "I would've growed," she said like a stubborn child. "He run off and left before I had a chance." Then she put her head down on her gnarled hands and began to cry. "I turned out purty," she said between sobs. "By the time I was thirteen I was the purtiest little thing on the island, but he was already gone. I waited for two more years before I married William, but he never come back 'til now." She wiped her eyes on her shawl and leaned her head back watching a spot on the ceiling. "He was too old for me then, and now it 'pears he's too young. After scatter-headed children

187

like you and Caroline. Oh, my blessed, what a cruel man."

What was I to do? For all the pain she had caused me, to see her like that, still haunted by a childish passion, made me want to put my arm around her and comfort her. But she had turned on me so often, I was afraid to touch her. I tried with words.

"I think he'd be glad to be your friend," I said. "He's all alone now." At least she seemed to be listening to me. "Call and Caroline and I used to go to see him. But—they are gone now, and it isn't proper for me to go down alone."

She raised her head. For a moment I was sure she was about to hurl one of her biblical curses at me, but she didn't. She just eased back and murmured something like "not proper."

So I took another bold step. "We could ask him for Christmas dinner," I said. "There'll be just the two of us. Wouldn't it seem more like Christmas to have company?"

"Would he be good?"

I wasn't sure what she meant by "good," but I said I was sure he would be.

"Can't have no yelling," she explained. "You can't have a body yelling at you when you're trying to eat."

"No," I said. "You can't have that." And added, "I'll tell him you said so."

She smiled slyly. "Yes," she said. "If he wants to come calling here, he better be good."

I wonder if I shall ever feel as old again as I did that

Christmas. My grandmother with her charm, gaudy and perishable as dime-store jewelry—whoever had a more exasperating child to contend with? The Captain responded with the dignity of a young teen who is being pestered by a child whose parents he is determined to impress. While I was the aged parent, weary of the tiresome antics of the one and the studied patience of the other.

But I shouldn't complain. Our dinner went remarkably well. I had a chicken—a great treat for us in those days—stuffed with oysters, boiled potatoes, corn pudding, some of Momma's canned beans, rolls, and a hot peach cobbler.

Grandma picked the oysters out of the stuffing and pushed them to the side of her plate. "You know I don't favor oysters," she said pouting at me.

"Oh, Miss Louise," said the Captain. "Try them with a bite of the white meat. They're delicious."

"It's all right," I said quickly. "Just leave them. Doesn't matter."

"I don't want them on my plate."

I jumped up and took her plate to the kitchen, scraped off the offending oysters, and brought it back, smiling as broadly as I could manage.

"How's that now?" I asked, sitting down.

"I don't favor corn pudding neither," she said. I hesitated, not sure if I should take the pudding off her plate or not. "But I'll eat it." She flashed a proud smile at the Captain. "A lot of times I eat things I don't really favor," she told him.

"Good," he said. "Good for you." He was beginning to relax a bit and enjoy his own dinner.

"Old Trudy died," she said after a while. Neither the Captain nor I replied to this. "Everybody dies," she said sadly.

"Yes, they do," he answered.

"I fear the water will get my coffin," she said. "I hate the water."

"You got some good years to go yet, Miss Louise."

She grinned at him saucily. "Longer than you anyway. I guess you wish now you was young as me, eh, Hiram Wallace?"

He put down his fork and patted his napkin to his beard. "Well—"

"One time I was too young and too poor for you to pay me any mind."

"I was a foolish young man, but that's a long time ago, now, Miss Louise."

"You had no cause to leave, you know. There was ones who would have had you, coward or no."

"Grandma? How about some more chicken?"

She was not to be distracted. "There's others who's not favored lightning, you know."

"Lightning?"

"'Course, chopping down your daddy's mast—" She tittered.

"That's just an old story, Grandma. The Captain never—"

"But I did," he said. "Took me twenty minutes to

chop it down and fifty years to set it back." He smiled at me, taking another roll from the tray I was offering. "It's so good to be old," he said. "Youth is a mortal wound."

"What's he talking about, Wheeze? I don't know what he's saying."

He put down his roll and reached over and took her gnarled hand, stroking the back of it with his thumb. "I'm trying to tell the child something only you and I can understand. How good it is to be old."

I watched her face go from being startled by his gesture to being pleased that he had somehow joined her side against me. Then she seemed to remember. She drew back her hand. "We'll die," she said.

"Yes," he said. "But we'll be ready. The young ones never are."

She would not leave us that day, even for her nap, but rocking in her chair after dinner, she fell asleep, her mouth slightly open, her head rolled awkwardly against her right shoulder.

I came in from washing the dishes to find the two of them in silence, she asleep and he watching her. "I thank you," I said. He looked up at me. "This would have been a lonesome day without you."

"I thank you," he said. And then, "It's hard for you, isn't it?"

I sat down on the couch near his chair. There was no need to pretend, I knew. "I had hoped when Call came home—"

He shook his head. "Sara Louise. You were never meant to be a woman on this island. A man, perhaps. Never a woman."

"I don't even know if I wanted to marry him," I said. "But I wanted something." I looked down at my hands. "I know I have no place here. But there's no escape."

"Pish."

"What?" I couldn't believe I'd heard him correctly.

"Pish. Rubbish. You can do anything you want to. I've known that from the first day I met you—at the other end of my periscope."

"But—"

"What is it you really want to do?"

I was totally blank. What was it I really wanted to do?

"Don't know?" It was almost a taunt. I was fidgeting under his gaze. "Your sister knew what she wanted, so when the chance came, she could take it."

I opened my mouth, but he waved me quiet. "You, Sara Louise. Don't tell me no one ever gave you a chance. You don't need anything given to you. You can make your own chances. But first you have to know what you're after, my dear." His tone was softening.

"When I was younger I wanted to go to boarding school in Crisfield—"

"Too late for that now."

"I—this sounds silly—but I would like to see the mountains."

"That's easy enough. Couple of hundred miles west is all." He waited, expecting more.

"I might—" the ambition began to form along with the sentence. "I want to be a doctor."

"So?" He was leaning forward, staring warmly at me. "So what's to stop you?"

Any answer would have been an excuse to him, the one I gave, most of all. "I can't leave them," I said, knowing he wouldn't believe me.

18

Two days after my parents' return from New York, I came the closest I ever came to fighting with my mother. Children raised as I was did not fight with their parents. There was even a commandment to take care of it, number five: "The only one of the Ten Commandments with a promise attached." I can still hear the preacher's twang as he lectured us. "Honor thy father and thy mother, that thy days may be long upon the land which the Lord thy God giveth thee."

When my mother got off the ferry, there was something different about her. At first I thought it was the hat. Caroline had bought her a new hat for the wedding, and she had worn it on the trip home. It was pale blue felt with a wide rolled-up brim that went out from her face at a slant. There was charm, both in the color, which exactly matched her eyes, and in the angle, which made her face look dramatic instead of simply thin. I could tell by looking at her how beautiful the hat made her feel. She was radiant. My father beside her looked proud and a little awkward in his Sunday suit. The sleeves had never been quite long enough to cover his brown wrists, and his huge weathered hands stuck out rather like the pinchers on a number one Jimmy.

They seemed glad enough to see me, but I could tell that they weren't quite ready to let go of their time together. I carried one of the suitcases and lagged behind them in the narrow street. Occasionally, one or the other of them would turn and smile at me to say something like "Everything go all right?" but they walked closer together than they needed to, touching each other as they walked every few steps and then smiling into each other's faces. My teeth rattled, I was shivering so.

Grandma was standing in the doorway waiting for us. They patted her as they went in. She seemed to sense at once whatever it was going on between them. Without a word of greeting she rushed to her chair, snatched up her Bible, and pushed the pages roughly and impatiently until she found the place she wanted.

" 'My son, give me thine heart, and let thine eyes observe my ways. For a whore is a deep ditch; and a strange woman is a narrow pit.' "

Momma's whole body shrank from the word "whore," but she recovered herself and went over to the umbrella stand where she carefully took the pins out of her hat. Her eyes steadily on her own image, she took off the hat, replaced the pins in the brim, and then patted her hair down with one hand. "There," she said, and taking one last look, turned from the mirror toward us. I was furious. Why didn't she scream? Grandma had no right—

"We'd best change," my father said and started up the stairs with the suitcases. She nodded and followed him up.

Grandma stood there, panting with frustration, all those words that she was bursting to say and no one but me to hear. Apparently, I would have to do. She glared at me and then began reading to herself as hastily as she could, searching, I suppose, for something she could fire at me and thus release her coiled spring.

"Here, Grandma," I said, my voice dripping molasses. "Let me help you." I'd been preparing for this moment for months. "Read it, here. Proverbs twenty-five, twenty-four." I flipped over and stuck my finger on the verse that I had memorized gleefully. " 'It is better,' " I recited piously, " 'to live in a corner of the housetop than in a house with a contentious woman.' " I smiled as sweetly as ever I knew how.

She snatched her Bible out from under my hand, slammed it shut, and holding it in both hands whacked me on the side of the head so hard that it was all I could do to keep from crying out. But at the same time I was glad that she hit me. Even while she stood there grinning at my surprise and pain, I felt a kind of satisfaction. I was deserving of punishment. I knew that. Even if I was not quite clear what I deserved it for.

But the incident didn't help Grandma. She was at my mother all the time now, following three steps behind her as she swept or cleaned, carrying the black Bible and reading and reciting to her. My father, meanwhile, seemed less than anxious to get the *Portia Sue* out on the Bay again. He spent several precious days happily tinkering with his engine, wasting lovely, almost warm, oyster weather. Couldn't he see how badly I needed to get away from that awful house? Couldn't he see that being cooped up with Grandma when she was going full throttle was driving me to the brink of insanity?

And my mother didn't help. Every waking moment was poisoned by Grandma's hatred, but my mother, head slightly bent as though heading into the wind, kept her silent course around the house with only a murmured word or two when a reply seemed necessary and could be given without risking further rancor. It would have been easier for me if she'd screamed or wept, but she didn't.

She did, however, propose that we wash the windows, a job we had done quite thoroughly at the end of the crab season. As I opened my mouth to protest, I saw her face and realized how much she needed to be outside the house, though she would never say so. I fetched the buckets of warm water and ammonia. We scrubbed and wiped in blessed silence for nearly a half hour. Through the porch window where I was working, I could see Grandma, poking anxiously about the living room. She wouldn't dare step out because of her arthritis, but it was clear that our peculiar behavior was disturbing to her. Watching her pinched face, I went through a spectrum of emotions. First a kind of perverted pride that my meek mother had bested the old woman, if only for an afternoon. Then a sort of nagging guilt that I should take such pleasure in my grandmother's discomfort. I could not forget that only the week before I had been touched by her childish griefs. This shifted to a growing anger that my clever, gentle, beautiful mother should be so unjustly persecuted, which was transformed, heaven knows how, into a fury against my mother for allowing herself to be so treated.

I moved my bucket and chair to the side of the house where she was standing on her chair, scrubbing and humming happily. "I don't understand it!" The words burst out unplanned.

"What, Louise?"

"You were smart. You went to college. You were good-looking. Why did you ever come here?"

She had a way of never seeming surprised by her children's questions. She smiled, not at me, but at some memory within herself. "Oh, I don't know," she said. "I was a bit of a romantic. I wanted to get away from what I thought of as a very conventional small town and try my wings." She laughed. "My first idea was to go to France."

"France?" I might not surprise her, but she could certainly surprise me.

"Paris, to be precise." She shook her head as she wrung out her rag over the bucket beside her on the chair. "It just shows how conventional I was. Everyone in my college generation wanted to go to Paris and write a novel."

"You wanted to go to Paris and write a novel?"

"Poetry, actually. I had published a few little things in college."

"You published poetry?"

"It's not as grand as it sounds. I promise you. Anyhow, my father wouldn't consider Paris. I didn't have the heart to defy him. My mother had just died." She added the last as though it explained her renunciation of Paris.

"You came to Rass instead of going to *Paris?*"

"It seemed romantic—" She began scrubbing again as she talked. "An isolated island in need of a schoolteacher. I felt—" She was laughing at herself. "I felt like one of the pioneer women, coming here. Besides—" She turned and looked at me, smiling at my incomprehension. "I had some notion that I would find myself here, as a poet, of course, but it wasn't just that."

The anger was returning. There was no good reason for me to be angry but my body was filled with it, the way it used to be when Caroline was home. "And did you find yourself here on this little island?" The question was coated with sarcasm.

She chose to ignore my tone. "I found very quickly," she scratched at something with her fingernail as she spoke, "I found there was nothing much to find."

I exploded. It was as though she had directly insulted me by speaking so slightingly of herself. "Why? Why did you throw yourself away?" I flung my rag into the bucket, sloshing gray ammonia water all over my ankles. Then I jumped from my chair and wrung out the rag as though it were someone's neck. "You had every chance in the world and you threw it all away for that—" and I jabbed my wrenched rag toward Grandma's face watching us petulantly from behind the glass.

"Please, Louise."

I turned so that I would not see either of their faces, a sob rising from deep inside me. I pounded on the side of the house to stop the tears, smashing out each syllable. "God in heaven, what a stupid waste."

She climbed off her chair and came over to me where I stood, leaning against the clapboard, shaking with tears of anger, grief—who knew what or for whom? She came round where I could see her, her arms halfway stretched out as though she would have liked to embrace me but dared not. I jumped aside. Did I think her touch would taint me? Somehow infect me with the weakness I perceived in her? "You could have done anything, been anything you wanted."

"But I am what I wanted to be," she said, letting her arms fall to her sides. "I chose. No one made me become what I am."

"That's sickening," I said.

"I'm not ashamed of what I have made of my life."

"Well, just don't try to make me like you are," I said. She smiled. "I can promise you I won't."

"I'm not going to rot here like Grandma. I'm going to get off this island and do something." I waited for her to stop me, but she just stood there. "You're not going to stop me, either."

"I wouldn't stop you," she said. "I didn't stop Caroline, and I certainly won't stop you."

"Oh, Caroline. Caroline's different. Everything's always been for Caroline. Caroline the delicate, the gifted, the beautiful. Of course, we must all sacrifice our lives to give her greatness to the world!"

Did I see her flinch, ever so slightly? "What do you want us to do for you, Louise?"

"Let me go. Let me leave!"

"Of course you may leave. You never said before you wanted to leave."

And, oh, my blessed, she was right. All my dreams of leaving, but beneath them I was afraid to go. I had clung to them, to Rass, yes, even to my grandmother, afraid that if I loosened my fingers an iota, I would find myself once more cold and clean in a forgotten basket.

"I chose the island," she said. "I chose to leave my own people and build a life for myself somewhere else. I certainly wouldn't deny you that same choice. But," and her eyes held me if her arms did not, "oh, Louise, we will miss you, your father and I."

I wanted so to believe her. "Will you really?" I asked. "As much as you miss Caroline?"

"More," she said, reaching up and ever so lightly smoothing my hair with her fingertips.

I did not press her to explain. I was too grateful for that one word that allowed me at last to leave the island and begin to build myself as a soul, separate from the long, long shadow of my twin.

19

Every spring a waterman starts out with brand clean crab pots. Crabs are particular critters, and they won't step into your little wire house if your bait is rank or your wire rusty and clogged with sea growth. But throw down a nice shiny pot with a bait box full of alewife that's just barely short of fresh, and they'll come swimming in the downstairs door, and before they know it they're snug in the upstairs and on the way to market.

That's the way I started out that spring. Shiny as a new crab pot, all set to capture the world. At my mother's suggestion, I wrote the county supervisor who had graded my high school exams, and he was happy to recommend me for a scholarship at the University of Maryland. My first thought was to stay home and help with the crabs until September. My father brushed the offer aside. I think my parents were afraid that if I didn't go at once, I'd lose my nerve. I wasn't worried about that, but I was eager to go, so I took off for College Park in April and got a room near the campus, waiting tables to pay my way until the summer session when I was able to move into the dormitory and begin my studies.

One day in the spring of my sophomore year, I found a note in my box directing me to see my advisor. It was a crisp, blue day that made me feel as I walked across the quadrangle that out near Rass the crabs were beginning to move. The air was fresh with the smell of new growth, and I went into that building and up to that office humming with the pure joy of being alive. I had forgotten that life, like a crab pot, catches a lot of trash you haven't bargained for.

"Miss Bradshaw." He cleaned his pipe, knocking it about the ashtray until I was ready to offer to clean it for him. "Miss Bradshaw. So."

He coughed and then elaborately refilled and lit his pipe.

"Yes, sir?"

He took a puff before going on. "I see you are doing well in your courses."

"Yes, sir."

"I suppose you are considering medicine."

"Yes, sir. That's why I'm in premed."

"I see." He puffed and sucked a bit. "You're serious about this? I would think that a good-looking young woman like you—"

"Yes, sir, I'm sure."

"Have you thought about nursing?"

"No, sir. I want to be a doctor."

When he saw how determined I was, he stopped fooling with his pipe. He wished it were different, he said, but with all the returning veterans, the chances of a girl, "even a bright girl like you" getting into medical school were practically nonexistent. He urged me to switch to nursing at the end of the semester.

A sea nettle hitting me in the face couldn't have stung worse. For a few days I was desolate, but then I decided that if you can't catch crabs where you are, you move your pots. I transferred to the University of Kentucky and into the nursing school, which had a good course in midwifery. I would become a nurse-midwife, spend a few years in the mountains where doctors were scarce, and then use my experience to persuade the government to send me to medical school on a public health scholarship.

When I was about ready to graduate, a list of Appalachian communities asking for nurse-midwives was posted on the student bulletin board. From the neat, double-spaced list, the name "Truitt" jumped out at me. When I was told the village was in a valley completely surrounded by mountains, the nearest hospital a two-hour drive over terrible roads, I was delighted. It seemed exactly the place for me to work for two or three years, see all the mountains I ever wanted to see, and then, armed with a bit of money and a lot of experience, to batter my way into medical school.

A mountain-locked valley is more like an island than anything else I know. Our water is the Appalachian wilderness, our boats, the army surplus jeeps we count on to navigate our washboard roads and the hairpin curves across the mountains. There are a few trucks, freely loaned about in good weather to any valley farmer who must take his pigs or calves to market. The rest of us seldom leave the valley.

The school is larger than the one on Rass, not only because there are twice the number of families, but because people here, even more than islanders, tend to count their wealth in children. There is a one-room Presbyterian Church, built of native stone, to which a preacher comes every three weeks when the road is passable. And every fourth Sunday, God and the weather willing, a Catholic priest says mass in the schoolhouse. There are no mines open in our pocket of western Virginia now, but the Polish and Lithuanian miners who were brought down from Pennsylvania two generations ago stayed and turned their hands to digging fields and cutting pastures out of the hillsides. They are still considered outsiders by the tough Scotch-Irish who have farmed the rocks of the valley floor for nearly two hundred years.

The most pressing health problem is one never encountered on Rass. On Saturday night, five or six of the valley men get blind drunk and beat their wives and children. In the Protestant homes I am told it is a Catholic problem, and in the Catholic homes, a Protestant. The truth, of course, is that the ailment crosses denominational lines. Perhaps it is the fault of the mountains, glowering above us, delaying sunrise and hastening the night. They are as awesome and beautiful as the open water, but the valley people do not seem to notice. Nor are they grateful for the game and timber that the mountains so generously provide. Most of them only see the ungiving soil from which a man must wrestle his subsistence and the barriers that shut him out from the world. These men struggle against their mountains. On Rass men followed the water. There is a difference.

Although the valley people are slow to accept outsiders, they did not hesitate to come to me. They needed my skill.

"Nurse?" An old ruddy-faced farmer was at my door in the middle of the night. "Nurse, would you be kind enough to see to my Betsy? She's having a bad go of it."

I dressed and went with him to his farm to deliver what I thought was a baby. To my amazement, he drove straight past the house to the barn. Betsy was his cow, but neither of us would have been prouder of that outsized calf had it been a child.

I came to wonder if every disease of man and beast had simply waited for my arrival to invade the valley. My little house, which was also the clinic, was usually jammed, and often there was a jeep waiting at the door to take me to examine a child or a cow or a woman in labor.

The first time I saw Joseph Wojtkiewicz (what my grandmother would have done to that name!), the first time I saw him to know who he was, that is, he arrived in his jeep late one night to ask me to come and treat his son, Stephen. Like most of the valley men, he seemed ill at ease with me, his only conversation during the ride was about the boy who had a severe earache and a fever of 105, which had made his father afraid to bring him out in the cold night air to the clinic.

The Wojtkiewicz house was a neatly built log cabin with four small rooms. There were three children, the six-year-old patient, and his two sisters, Mary and Anna, who were eight and five. The mother had been dead for several years.

The county had sent me an assortment of drugs including a little penicillin, so I was able to give the child a shot. Then an alcohol rubdown to bring the fever down a bit until the drug had time to do its work, a little warm oil to soothe the ear, a word or two to commend bravery, and I was ready to go.

I had repacked my bag and was heading for the door when I realized the boy's father had made coffee for me. It seemed rude not to drink it, so I sat opposite him at his kitchen table, my face set in my most professional smile, mouthing reassurance and unnecessary directions for the child's care.

I became increasingly aware that the man was staring at me, not impolitely, but as though he were studying an unknown specimen. At last he said, "Where do you come from?"

"The University of Kentucky," I said. I prided myself on never letting remarks made by patients or their families surprise me.

"No, no," he said. "Not school. Where do you really come from?"

I began to tell him quite matter-of-factly about Rass, where it was, what it looked like, slipping into a picture of how it had been. I hadn't returned to the island since entering nursing school except for two funerals, my grandmother's and the Captain's. Now as I described the marsh as it was when I was a child, I could almost feel the wind on my arms and hear the geese baying like a pack of hounds as they flew over. No one on the mainland had ever invited me to talk about home before, and the longer I talked, the more I wanted to talk, churning with happiness and homesickness at the same time.

The little girls had come into the kitchen and were leaning on either side of their father's chair, listening with the same dark-eyed intensity. Joseph put an arm around each of them, absently stroking the black curls of Anna who was on his right.

At last I stopped, a little shy for having talked so much. I even apologized.

"No, no," he said. "I asked because I wanted to know. I knew there was something different about you. I kept wondering ever since you came. Why would a woman like you, who could have anything she wanted, come to a place like this? Now I understand." He left off stroking his daughter's hair and leaned forward, his big hands open as though he needed their help to explain his meaning. "God in heaven,"—I thought at first it was an oath, it had been so long since I'd heard the expression used in any other way—"God in heaven's been raising you for this valley from the day you were born."

I was furious. He didn't know anything about me or the day I was born or he'd never say such a foolish thing, sitting there so piously at his kitchen table, sounding for all the world like a Methodist preacher.

But then, oh, my blessed, he smiled. I guess from that moment I knew I was going to marry Joseph Wojtkiew-icz—God, pope, three motherless children, unspellable surname and all. For when he smiled, he looked like the kind of man who would sing to the oysters.

20

It is far simpler to be married to a Catholic than anyone from my Methodist past would believe. I am quite willing for the children, his, of course, but also ours as they come along, to be raised in the Catholic faith. The priest frets about me when we meet, but he's only around once a month, and Joseph himself has never suggested that I ought to turn Catholic or even religious. My parents showed their approval by making the long trip from Rass to attend our schoolhouse wedding. I will always be glad that my father and Joseph met each other that once, because this year, on the second of October, my father went to sleep in his chair after a day of crabbing and never woke up.

Caroline called me from New York. I couldn't remember ever having heard her cry aloud before, and there she was weeping for the benefit of the entire Truitt village party line. I was unreasonably irritated. She and Call were going down at once and would stay through the funeral. It seemed wrong that she should be able to go and not me. I was the child who had fished his crab floats and culled his oysters, but I was so far along in my ninth month that I knew better than anyone how crazy it would be to try such a trip; so Joseph went in my place and got back to the farm four days before our son was born.

We thought he might bring Momma back with him then, but Caroline was making her New Haven debut as Musetta in *La Bohème* on the twenty-first. Our parents had planned to go before my father's death, so Caroline and Call begged her to return with them and stay on through the opening. Since she would be coming to live with us soon, it seemed the right thing for her to do. Joseph did not plead my condition. He was already learning midwifery, and I think my mother understood that he would have been disappointed not to deliver our child himself.

I suppose every mother is reduced to idiocy when describing her firstborn, but, oh, he is a beauty—large and dark like his father, but with the bright blue eyes of the Bradshaws. I swear from his cry that he will be a singer and from his huge hands that he will follow the water, which makes his father laugh aloud and tease me about our son setting sail on the trickle of a stream that crosses our pasture.

The older children adore him, and, as for the valley people, it doesn't matter how often I explain that we named the baby for my father, they are all sure that

Truitt is their namesake. Their need for me made them accept me into their lives, but now I feel that they are taking me into their hearts as well.

My work did not, could not, end with my marriage to Joseph and his children or even with the birth of Truitt. There is no one else to care for the valley. The hospital remains two hours away, and the road is impassable for much of the winter.

This year our winter came early. In November I was watching over two pregnancies, one of which I worried about. The mother is a thin, often-beaten girl of about eighteen. From the size of her, I quickly suspected twins and urged her and her husband to go to the hospital in Staunton or Harrisonburg for the delivery.

Despite his bouts of drunkenness, the young husband is well-meaning. He would have taken her, I believe, had there been any money at all. But how could I urge them to make the trip when the hospital might well reject her? And without money where could they stay in the city until the babies actually came? I counted the days and measured her progress as best I could and then sent word to a doctor in Staunton that I would need help with the births. But it snowed twenty inches the day before Essie went into labor, so when they called me, I went alone.

The first twin, a nearly six-pound boy, came fairly easily, despite Essie's slender frame, but the second did not follow as I thought it should. I had begun to fear for it, when I realized that it was very small, but in a breach position. I reached in and turned the twin so that she was delivered head first, but blue as death. Before I even cut the cord, I put my mouth down and breathed into her tiny one. Her chest, smaller than my fist, shuddered, and she gave a cry, but so weak, so like a parting, that I was near despair.

"Is it all right?" Essie asked.

"Small," I said and busied myself cutting and tying off the cord. How cold she was. It sent painful shivers up my arms. I called the grandmother, who had been taking care of the boy, to get me blankets and see to the afterbirth.

I swathed the child tightly and held her against my body. It was like cuddling a stone. I almost ran from the bedroom. What was I to do? They must give me an incubator if they expected me to care for newborn babies in this godforsaken place.

The kitchen was slightly warmer than the bedroom. I went over to the enormous iron stove. A remnant of a fire was banked in the far corner under the stove top. I put my hand on the stove and found it comfortingly warm. I grabbed an iron pot, stuffed it with all the dish-rags and towels I could reach with one hand, lay the baby in it, and set it in the oven door. Then I pulled up a kitchen stool and sat there with my hand on the baby's body and watched. It may have been hours. I was too intent to keep track, but, at length, a sort of pinkness invaded the translucent blue skin of her cheek.

"Nurse?" I jumped at the sound. The young father

had come into the kitchen. "Nurse, should I go for the priest?" His eyes widened at the sight of the nurse cooking his baby in the oven, but, rather than protest, he repeated his question about fetching the priest.

"How could you on these roads?" I'm sure I sounded impatient. I wanted to be left in peace to guard my baby.

"Should I do it myself?" he asked, apparently alarmed by whatever it was he was suggesting. "Or you could."

"Oh, do be quiet."

"But, Nurse, it must be baptized before it dies."

"She won't die!"

He flinched. I'm sure he found me terrifying. "But, if it did—"

"She will not die." But to keep him quiet and get rid of him, I poured water out of the cold teakettle onto my hand and reached into the oven, placing my hand on the blur of dark hair. "What is her name?"

He shook his head in bewilderment. Apparently, everything was left for me to do. Susan. Susan was the name of a saint, wasn't it? Well, if not, they could have the priest fix it later. "Essie Susan," I said, "I baptize you in the name of the Father and of the Son and of the Holy Ghost. Amen." Under my hand the tiny head stirred.

The father crossed himself, nodded a scared-rabbit kind of thank you, and hurried out to report the sacrament to his wife. Soon the grandmother was in the kitchen.

"Thank you, Nurse. We're grateful to you."

"Where is the other twin?" I asked, suddenly stricken.

I had forgotten him. In my anxiety for his sister, I had completely forgotten him. "Where have you put him?"

"In the basket." She looked at me, puzzled. "He's sleeping."

"You should hold him," I said. "Hold him as much as you can. Or let his mother hold him."

She started for the door. "Nurse. Should I baptize him as well?"

"Oh, yes," I said. "Baptize him and then let Essie nurse him."

My own breasts were swollen with milk for Truitt. I knew his father would bring him to me soon, but there was plenty. I took my baby out of the oven and held her mouth to catch the milk, which began to flow of its own accord. A perfect tongue, smaller than a newborn kitten's, reached out for the drops of milk on her lips. Then the little mouth rooted against my breast until she had found the nipple for herself.

Hours later, walking home, my boots crunching on the snow, I bent my head backward to drink in the crystal stars. And clearly, as though the voice came from just behind me, I heard a melody so sweet and pure that I had to hold myself to keep from shattering:

I wonder as I wander out under the sky . . .

Katherine Paterson's works have received wide acclaim. Among them are *Bridge to Terabithia,* winner of the 1978 Newbery Medal; *The Great Gilly Hopkins,* a Newbery Honor Book and winner of the 1979 National Book Award; and *The Master Puppeteer,* awarded the 1977 National Book Award.

Katherine Paterson was born in China, the daughter of missionary parents, and spent part of her childhood there. She was educated in both China and the United States, graduating from King College, in Bristol, Tennessee, and later receiving her master's degree in English Bible from the Presbyterian School of Christian Education in Richmond, Virginia. She lived in Japan for four years, working for two of those years as a Christian Education Assistant to a group of eleven pastors in rural Japan.

Her four children and their friends have provided her with some of the subject matter for her sharply observant stories of family life. She lives with them and her husband in Norfolk, Virginia.

Paterson, Katherine
Jacob have I loved.

        JW